Race
–for the–
Record

Trailblazer Books

Hero Tales: A Family Treasury of True Stories
From the Lives of Christian Heroes (Volumes I, II, III, & IV)

*Curriculum guide available.
Written by Julia Pferdehirt with Dave & Neta Jackson.

Race
–for the–
Record

Dave & Neta Jackson

Story illustrations by
Julian Jackson

BETHANY HOUSE PUBLISHERS
MINNEAPOLIS, MINNESOTA 55438

Race for the Record
Copyright © 1999
Dave and Neta Jackson

Illustrations © 1999
Bethany House Publishers

Story illustrations by Julian Jackson.
Cover design and illustration by Catherine Reishus McLaughlin.

Scripture quotations are from the King James Version of the Bible.

Published by Bethany House Publishers
A Ministry of Bethany Fellowship International
11400 Hampshire Avenue South
Minneapolis, Minnesota 55438
www.bethanyhouse.com

Printed in the United States of America by
Bethany Press International, Minneapolis, Minnesota 55438

Library of Congress Cataloging-in-Publication Data

Jackson, Dave.
    Race for the record / Dave & Neta Jackson.
       p. cm. — (Trailblazer books)
    Twelve-year-old Alastair, a son of Christian missionaries on the
Philippine island of Palawan, finds a way for Joy Ridderhof to
record the Gospels in the native language.
    ISBN 0–7642–2013–6 (pbk.)
    [1. Missionaries Fiction. 2. Christian life Fiction.
3. Palawan (Philippines) Fiction. 4. Island—Philippines Fiction.
5. Ridderhof, Joy, Fiction.] I. Jackson, Neta. II. Title.
III. Series: Jackson, Dave. Trailblazer books.
PZ7.J132418 Rac 1999
[Fic]—dc21   99–6538
                                                       CIP

All the known facts about Joy Ridderhof's visit to Brooke's Point on Palawan Island are included in this story—Bert Edwards' dream during World War II; the eager preparations of the Sutherland and Edwards families for Joy Ridderhof's visit; the recorder that would not work; and Lastani's last-minute appearance in Puerto Princesa so that the recordings could be made.

However, the only thing we know about the *real* Alastair Sutherland, the young son of the Scottish pastor at Brooke's Point, is that he was recovering from malaria when Joy Ridderhof and her companion arrived in August 1950. And the only thing we know about the *real* Lastani is that he was the Palawanos boy who was going to do the translation work but had to leave for the Farm School before Joy Ridderhof arrived. We have taken liberties to give both Alastair and Lastani "fictional stories" in order to tell this story through their eyes. (*Note:* An unnamed passenger Joy Ridderhof met on the steamer on the return trip to Puerto Princesa was the actual person who went to the Farm School and brought Lastani to Mr. Alvior's house.)

Certain facts regarding Joy Ridderhof's travels in the Philippines—e.g., the man with the good-luck charm, the Muslim who didn't want to listen to the gospel records—have been worked into the happenings at Brooke's Point to give a fuller picture of the work of Gospel Recordings.

Find us on the Web at . . .

trailblazerbooks.com

- Meet the authors.

- Read the first chapter of each book—with the pictures.

- Track the Trailblazers around the world on a map.

- Use the historical timeline to find out what other important events were happening in the world at the time of each Trailblazer story.

- Discover how the authors research their books and link to some of the same sources they used where you can learn more about these heroes.

- Write to the authors.

- Explore frequently asked questions about the Trailblazer books and being writers.

Just point your browser to http://www.trailblazerbooks.com

CONTENTS

DAVE AND NETA JACKSON are a full-time husband/wife writing team who have authored and coauthored many books on marriage and family, the church, relationships, and other subjects. Their books for children include the TRAILBLAZER series and *Hero Tales* volumes I, II, and III. The Jacksons have two married children, Julian and Rachel, and make their home in Evanston, Illinois.

Chapter 1

The Forest Hideout
(Palawan Island, Philippines, 1942)

FOUR-YEAR-OLD ALASTAIR clung tightly to his daddy's broad shoulders as Sandy Sutherland scrambled up the steep footpath. "Hang on, laddie," said his father. "We're almost to the clearing."

Alastair looked back and saw his mother struggling up the rocky path behind them, carrying two-year-old Heather on her hip.

"Will Bertie be there?" asked Alastair, ducking his head to avoid some big ferns along the path.

His father hesitated just a moment before saying softly, "By God's guid graces, aye, laddie."

Because of "the war," the Sutherlands and their friends the Edwardses had been living for months in the rain forest that covered the mountains on Palawan Island. Six months earlier, just before Christmas, the news had crackled on the radio: The Japanese had dropped bombs on Manila, the capital city of the Philippine Islands—right after bombing American ships at Pearl Harbor, Hawaii. *"America has declared war on Japan!"* the radio announcer sputtered. *"The war in Europe has become World War II!"*

Alastair's parents, Sandy and Maisie Sutherland, were Scottish Brethren missionaries who pastored a little church in the isolated town of Brooke's Point on Palawan Island. Harry Edwards was an American businessman who lived in Brooke's Point with his Filipino wife and their just-graduated-from-college son, Bertie. But with the bombing of Manila—even though Manila was five hundred miles away on Luzon, the largest of the Philippine Islands—the Sutherlands and Edwardses realized their lives were in danger. The two families rolled clothes and food into bundles and fled into the mountain forests.

Alastair squeezed his eyes shut and laid his head against his father's warm back. He didn't understand war. He didn't understand why they had to live in the forest, moving from barrio to barrio, sleeping on the ground instead of in his own nice bed. The people in the different villages sometimes shared their rice and fish, but Alastair always felt hungry. He wanted to go home.

But today was Sunday, and by agreement the

Sutherland and the Edwards families tried to meet on the Lord's Day for a time of worship and encouragement. The trail broke through a tangle of lacy ferns, vines, and bright tropical flowers and opened into a small clearing. A tall man in his sixties, standing at the edge of the clearing where the forest fell away sharply down to the sea, looked through a pair of binoculars.

Harry Edwards turned and gave a brief, tired smile as the Scottish family came and stood beside him. "You heard?" said the American.

"Aye," said Sandy Sutherland. "The Japanese defeated the Americans at Corregidor Island. It's . . . only a matter of time now."

Alastair peeked over his father's shoulder. The town of Brooke's Point lay below them, caught like a pearl between the bright blue waters of the Sulu Sea and the steep mountains that ran like a bony spine down the length of Palawan Island. The bay was empty. Alastair remembered watching the *vintas*, or outrigger fishing canoes, go out each evening, their colorful sails muted by the long shadows cast by the mountains. Even more exciting was the occasional steamboat that traveled from island to island, bringing passengers or picking up sacks of bananas, coconuts, bamboo, rattan, and almaciga gum to sell in the cities. But no steamships had come to Brooke's Point for months.

The sandy-haired four-year-old wiggled down from his perch on his father's back. "Where's Bertie?" he piped up; then he saw the young man, who was in his early twenties, half sitting up with his back against a coconut palm at the edge of the clearing. Mrs. Edwards, her long dark hair swept up into a knot on the back of her head, knelt beside her son, mopping Bert's sweaty face.

Bert Edwards was Filipino-American. A year ago he had graduated from the University of Illinois in the United States with a degree in farming. He had come home to Palawan Island full of ideas how to help the mountain tribespeople grow more food. But Alastair was worried about his friend, who was kind of like a big brother. Bertie had been sick with malaria twice already since he got home from college, and he looked very sick again.

"Hey, Ali," Bert said with a weak grin as the little boy hunched down beside him. "How's my buddy?"

"How are *you*, Bertie, is more like it," said Alastair's father as the rest of the Sutherland family and Harry Edwards also came over to the tree Bert was propped against.

Bert rolled his feverish eyes mockingly. "Never better," he joked—and then was overcome by a fit of coughing.

"He's got blackwater fever now, Pastor!" said Mrs. Edwards desperately. "We don't have any quinine to give him, no dry clothes—we can't keep going!"

"Mama . . . please," Bert begged. "It's all right. I need to talk to the pastor about something."

Sandy Sutherland crouched down next to Alastair and rested an arm on one knee. "Aye, Bert, what is it?"

Bert tried to take a large breath. "Remember . . .

remember when I was telling you all my grand ideas about teaching the mountain tribespeople modern ways to grow more food? You said, 'They also need spiritual food, Bert. But they have no written language, no Bible. How—'" The young man stopped, exhausted. After a few moments he went on. "'How are they going to learn about Jesus?' you said."

Sandy Sutherland nodded. It was true. On Palawan Island alone there were eighty-seven different dialects among the mountain tribespeople.

Bert managed another grin. "Well, I've got an idea. At college the guys and gals listened to records all the time and knew the words to all the songs they listened to. Why not . . . why not make gospel records in . . . in the Palawano language, for instance. Most of the tribes know some Palawano—they use it for trading with each other. If every barrio had a record player and some gospel records, they could hear the Gospel, even if they can't read!"

Alastair saw his father and Mr. Edwards exchange surprised glances. "That is quite an idea, Bertie," Sandy Sutherland said. "I wonder how . . ."

Alastair sighed and got to his feet. It just wasn't the same since they'd been hiding in the forest. Nobody laughed and played anymore. Bertie used to throw him up in the air and let him ride on his back, like a pony. If only they could go home and live in Brooke's Point again, Bertie would get well, and things would be like they used to be.

Alastair wandered over to the far side of the clearing and looked down the mountainside at the

town far below. Then he saw something out on the
bay. Specks moving toward shore . . .

"Papa! Mr. Edwards!" the little boy cried out, pointing down toward the bay. "I see boats! The fishermen are coming back! The fishermen are coming back!"

In a few strides Harry Edwards and Sandy Sutherland had crossed the clearing. The American peered intently at the specks on the bright blue water with his binoculars. "Those aren't fishing boats," he said, handing the binoculars to the missionary. "What do you think, Sandy?"

Alastair's father looked long and hard through the glasses. Then he lowered them. "Soldiers," he said. "Japanese. Some of them have landed already and are going house to house."

"Mummy!" whimpered two-year-old Heather.

Maisie Sutherland scooped up the little girl in her arms. "Oh, Sandy! We can'na stay here. We have to go farther up the mountain. But—" She looked back toward the sick young man under the coconut tree. "But what about Bert?"

Frightened, Alastair looked from his father to his mother to Mr. Edwards and back again. What was happening? Why was everyone so upset all of a sudden?

"Don't worry about us," said Harry Edwards firmly. "You folks go on ahead. We'll be all right."

"No one's gaing anywhere until we have our ain worship together," said Sandy Sutherland firmly. "That's what we came fer, and that'll be what we do."

The two small families gathered under the leafy palm branches of the coconut tree. Sandy Sutherland took his Bible out of his pocket and turned to the book of Habakkuk. " 'Although the fig tree shall not blossom,' " he read in his rich Scottish voice, " 'neither shall fruit be in the vines . . . the flock shall be cut off from the fold, and there shall be no herd in the stalls: Yet I will rejoice in the LORD! . . . The LORD God is my strength, and he will make my feet like hinds' feet, and he will make me to walk upon mine high places.' "

"What does 'like hinds' feet' mean?" Alastair whispered loudly, tugging on his father's arm.

"It means like the nimble feet of a deer bounding up a mountainside," Sandy Sutherland said with a chuckle. "A guid Scripture for our situation, don'na ya think?"

"Yes," said Maisie Sutherland softly. Little Heather's curly head was buried in her neck. "Even though nothing is going right, we will still rejoice in the Lord."

Sandy Sutherland again knelt on one knee beside the sick young man. "Bert," said the missionary pastor gently, "the Japanese have landed at Brooke's Point. We don't have much time to be together this mornin'. But do ya have a favorite song ye'd like us to sing?"

Bert's feverish eyes burned bright. " 'Count Your Blessings'—please sing that one."

The missionary pastor smiled at Bert's choice. His deep, baritone voice started on the first verse, and the others joined in . . .

"When upon life's billow
you are tempest tossed,
When you are discouraged
thinking all is lost;
Count your many blessings,
name them one by one,
And it will surprise you
what the Lord hath done!"

The little group couldn't help smiling at one another as they belted out the chorus: " 'Count your blessings! Name them one by one! . . .' "

✧ ✧ ✧ ✧

No little group gathered in the mountain clearing overlooking the Sulu Sea the following Sunday. But under the coconut palm was a freshly dug grave.

Down in the town of Brooke's Point, the Japanese soldiers had set up camp, taking over the pleasant homes of the Edwardses and the Sutherlands for their headquarters. At the end of a street lined by pretty little bamboo houses on stilts, the sturdy chapel was empty.

Somewhere deep in the forest, two families—one American, one Scottish—climbed farther up the mountains, not knowing if they'd ever see their homes again. And even though they'd lost someone dear to all of them, there was a song in their hearts that they hummed and whispered to encourage one another: "Count your blessings, name them one by one. . . ."

Chapter 2

The Gum Gatherers
(Seven years later, 1949, Palawan Island)

ALASTAIR SUTHERLAND UNBUTTONED HIS SHIRT collar and slumped against the plain wooden pew of the little chapel in Brooke's Point. At eleven years of age, he was expected to sit through his father's sermons without wiggling, but it was so hot! The air seemed trapped inside the whitewashed wooden chapel, without even a sea breeze passing through the open windows to nudge it.

April and May were the hottest months in the Philippine Islands. Hot and dry. At least school was out until June; that's when the monsoon rains started. School ... Alastair silently groaned. He was tired of going to the little Christian school here in Brooke's

18

Point. The school didn't even have a building; it met in the chapel. Only two teachers—and one was Alastair's own mother. He wanted to go to the boarding school in Manila with the children of other foreign missionaries. But no—his parents said he had to wait until he was twelve years old, which meant he had to wait another whole year.

Alastair sighed. At least his parents had said he was old enough to go along with his father and Mr. Edwards on Mr. Edwards' next trading trip into the mountains—and they were going tomorrow. He glanced across the aisle at the gray-haired American businessman sitting with his sweet Filipino wife. The Edwardses' son, Bertie, used to go with his father on these trips into the mountains of Palawan Island—but that was before Bertie had died of blackwater fever during the war.

Bertie Edwards . . . Alastair could hardly remember the young man who used to be like a big brother to him and his little sister, Heather. In fact, he could hardly remember the two years his family and the Edwards family spent hiding in the mountains. But he did remember the American submarine that had rescued them from the island when he was six years old. The U.S. Navy had taken them to a hospital in Australia to recover from their ordeal.

When the war was over a few months later, though, the Sutherlands had come right back to Palawan Island to continue their missionary work. How glad they were when Mr. and Mrs. Edwards returned safely home to Brooke's Point, too! Even though Harry Edwards' storage sheds and trade goods had been destroyed during the war, he started over, building up his export business. Soon he was once again taking trips up the mountain trails to trade for the gum resin, beeswax, and rattan reeds that the Palawanos tribespeople collected from the forest. These raw materials could be sold in the cities, where they were made into all sorts of useful things like paint and plastic and polish and furniture.

Sometimes Alastair's father, Sandy Sutherland, went along with Harry Edwards on these trips, hoping to make contact with some of the tribespeople to tell them about Jesus. But most of them spoke only Palawano; only a few knew Tagalog, the trade language of the Philippines that Mr. Edwards had learned.

Alastair had always liked to hear stories about these trips. Mr. Edwards told him about the gum gatherers, young men and boys who climbed the towering almaciga palms to collect the gum resin. They scurried up ropes of twisted vines like circus acrobats. But now Alastair would get to see these daredevils for himself . . . if he didn't suffocate from heat right here in the church pew first.

Alastair eyed the pulpit. How long was his father going to preach? He wished he had a fan. Then he noticed a Sunday school paper sticking out of the Bible on his mother's lap. *Just right for making a paper fan.* He looked at her sideways, wondering if she'd mind if he used it, but Maisie Sutherland was busy trying to corral his two wiggly little brothers, Glen and Craigie. His sister, nine-year-old Heather, sat as far away at the end of the pew as she could get.

Carefully, Alastair pinched a corner of the Sunday school paper and pulled it slowly out of his mother's Bible. Success! She hadn't noticed. He opened the paper to make a bigger fan and began to fold it, accordion-like. But some words in big type on the inside page caught his eye: "Missionary Takes Gospel Records to Primitive Tribes."

Alastair stopped folding. Gospel records? Wasn't that what his father and Mr. Edwards talked about sometimes? They said it had been Bertie Edwards' idea—making records in the Palawano language so even people who couldn't read could hear stories about Jesus. Now here was somebody who was doing that very thing!

Just then Alastair's father announced the last hymn. Finally! When the service was over, Alastair quickly slipped off the wooden bench and ran outside. People were starting to walk or ride their bicycles down the lane between the rows of neat bamboo houses perched on six-foot stilts. Bushes lush with purple and red bougainvillea flowers ran riot between the thatched roof houses. Alastair looked this way and that. Had he missed Mr. Edwards already?

Then he saw him and his wife walking down the lane. "Mr. Edwards!" he cried, running after them. "Look at this." As the older couple turned, the sandy-haired boy shoved the Sunday school paper into the older man's hands.

"What is it, son?" said Harry Edwards. As he

quickly scanned the story, a boyish grin spread across his face. Without another word, the tall American—still spry at age seventy—sprinted back toward the chapel with Alastair in hot pursuit.

Sandy Sutherland had finished shaking hands with people as they came out of the chapel and was shutting the doors when Harry Edwards and Alastair found him. "Look here, Sandy," Harry Edwards said, waving the Sunday school paper in the pastor's face. "Someone else had the same idea Bertie did—and is actually doing it!"

Sandy Sutherland scanned the story. "Joy Ridderhof, hmm . . . started her ain mission called Gospel Recordings. Look . . . Says here that she's made recordings of primitive languages in Honduras and Mexico and Alaska . . . and now those isolated people have the Gospel on records. Amazing!" He looked up from the paper. "I wonder . . . do you think Gospel Recordings would send someone here?"

Harry Edwards slapped his friend on the shoulder. "That's what we're going to ask them!" he laughed. "I'll write Miss Ridderhof today. Wouldn't it be fantastic if someone from Gospel Recordings would come to Brooke's Point?—though how we'd get their recording equipment up the mountain, I can't even begin to imagine."

Alastair, who was following the two men as they talked, silently agreed. He knew his father and Mr. Edwards were excited about this record idea—but it did seem slightly crazy. After all, most of the mountain tribes didn't let strangers come into their barrios—he'd heard that often enough. They were afraid of the strange sicknesses that foreigners brought with them. Tomorrow, for instance, they would hike up the trail to a "trading spot" where the forest people were willing to meet to trade their goods. But if they tried to go to their villages uninvited, they might get shot with blowguns.

Besides, he snorted to himself, how would the mountain people play the records? They didn't even have electricity!

❖ ❖ ❖ ❖

A thin ribbon of gray light was just beginning to separate the horizon into sea and sky when Alastair's father shook his shoulder the next morning. "Time to get up, lad. Make it quick. We don't want to keep Mr. Edwards waiting." Alastair opened one eye. Why was his father waking him up so early? The sun wasn't even up yet.

Then he remembered. Today was the day he was going on a trading trip up the mountains!

By the time Alastair and his father got down to the beach where Mr. Edwards' crew was loading a jeepney with metal pots, bolts of cloth, and sacks of salt and rice, the rising sun was cutting a blazing path across the Sulu Sea. The sky was cloudless; tall coconut palms lining the pearl-white beach waved their long fronds like a welcome in the early morning breeze.

"Swing on board!" called out Mr. Edwards, hopping into the driver's seat of the jeepney. "We'll drive this stuff as far as the trailhead, then hike it up the rest of the way."

An hour later, the trading party was well on their way up the mountain trail. Ten strong, wiry porters—Filipinos employed by Mr. Edwards—carried the goods for trading on their shoulders or backs. Alastair scrambled up the rocky path, trying to keep up. The forest was so thick with ivy, ferns, and walls of morning glory leaves that the light filtering through the treetops was dim and gloomy.

The hikers stopped midmorning to drink from their canteens and rest for fifteen minutes. "How do you think this Joy Ridderhof does it?" Alastair heard his father say to Harry Edwards as they munched on the nuts and dried fruit Maisie Sutherland had packed for them. "I mean, we'd have to find someone who could translate from English into Tagalog, and then someone else who could translate Tagalog into Palawano—and even then, how would we know the translation was'na all mixed up?"

Mr. Edwards chuckled. "You're the preacher, Sutherland. I'm the one who should be asking the doubting-Thomas questions."

Sandy Sutherland laughed. "You're right," he said, rolling his r's in his soft Scottish accent. "I should have more faith. Finding that story about Gospel Recordings was'na a coincidence, was it—more like a miracle, ay?"

Alastair sighed. His father and Mr. Edwards were acting like that Joy lady was coming next week! The letter wouldn't even go out until the next steamer came to Brooke's Point. And even when she got the letter, she might not be able to send anyone to the Philippines. It was a long shot, for sure.

It was almost noon when the trading party came to a fork in the trail. "Unload here!" Mr. Edwards called to the porters. He waved a hand at a small area that had been cleared of brush and vines.

"But . . . there's no one here," said Alastair, looking around in disappointment. He had hoped to see some of the mountain people.

"They know we're here. Just wait," said his father quietly.

They waited. The men mopped their necks with big bandannas. Insects whined. Bored, Alastair watched a bright yellow-and-black butterfly rest on a cluster of orchids that wrapped like a collar around a tree trunk. Then it flitted away. As Alastair followed it with his eyes, he saw a small man standing stock-still in the middle of the trail just above them. He was naked except for a loincloth of bark around his waist. His long black hair was bundled up at the back of his head.

"Papa!" he whispered loudly. How long had the man been there?

"*Apo*—hello," said Mr. Edwards, getting to his feet.

"Apo," said the man, suddenly smiling, showing a row of teeth darkened by betel-nut juice. He spit, then smiled again.

Mr. Edwards motioned to his foreman, José, who was fluent in Tagalog, to help him talk to the man. The tall American seemed to tower over the short tribesman, who gestured up one fork of the trail. After a few brief exchanges in Tagalog and Palawano, José said, "He wants us to follow him to where they're gathering the almaciga gum. We can trade there."

The trail now seemed steeper and harder. Sometimes Alastair couldn't even see that there *was* a trail. But he doggedly followed his father's back through the huge elephant leaves and vines.

Soon they heard voices chattering to one another. The voices seemed nearby, but Alastair couldn't see anyone. Then a movement caught his eye in the palm trees towering above him. He tipped his head back and looked up.

Rattan vines had been strung at a steep angle between several trees—anchored low on one tree, then tied halfway up a second tall palm. Another vine then went back, higher now, to the first tree, while still another vine strung upward to a third tree. Young men and boys were climbing up these taut, slanted vines, pulling themselves hand over hand while their feet ran up the vines like tightrope walkers.

Now everywhere Alastair looked, he saw limber young boys and men climbing the taut vines into the towering palms. They called back and forth to each other, laughing, filling slings that they wore over their shoulders with the precious gummy resin.

"Apo! Apo!" they called down to the trading party on the ground, and then they laughed.

By now the porters in the trading party had put down the sacks they had carried up the mountainside. They unloaded some of the items, then refilled the sacks with raw almaciga gum. Alastair sat on a rock out of the way, watching all the activity. Ten yards away he noticed a slender boy—maybe fifteen years old—arguing with a man. The boy kept pointing at a piece of carved bone that hung on a leather string around the man's neck, then pointing to himself. The man shook his head and gestured angrily up into the trees. Protesting, the boy grabbed the leather string, but the man hit his hand away.

Alastair looked questioningly at Mr. Edwards. "What's happening?"

Harry Edwards watched the tussle for a moment. "Looks like the boy wants the man's necklace—probably a good-luck charm of some kind."

"But why?" asked Alastair.

"I'm not sure," said Mr. Edwards. "But the Palawanos are very afraid of evil spirits. They have all sorts of rituals and chants and charms to protect themselves."

Finally the man grabbed the boy's arm and again pointed up into the trees. Jerking his arm away, the Palawanos boy angrily shouted something and scurried like a monkey up one of the rattan vines. The man stalked away.

Alastair's stomach growled. Come to think of it, he hadn't had anything to eat since they stopped to rest at midmorning. It must be afternoon by now. He knew his mother had packed some food for him and his father. He rummaged in a pack. Where was that food...?

A scream made him jump. Jerking his head, Alastair saw the boy who had been arguing with—

who, his father?—falling from the tree he'd been climbing. The boy grabbed frantically at some loose vines, but they just pulled away in his hand; he dropped like a stone, landing in a bushy thicket with a sickening thud.

Chapter 3

The Jeweled Knife

THE TEENAGE BOY LAY STILL, crumpled in the bushes. The man with the leather necklace looked frightened. He began to wail and moan, slapping his chest and tugging on the small piece of carved bone hanging around his neck.

Talking excitedly, the other gum gatherers began to crowd around the spot where the boy had fallen.

"Wait! Don'na move him!" Sandy Sutherland yelled, holding up his hand. The Palawanos didn't understand the missionary pastor's words, but they understood his tone of voice.

Frightened, Alastair

watched his father scramble into the bushes and feel for the boy's pulse. Was the boy dead? What happened? Why did he fall off the vine?

"He's alive," Sandy Sutherland said. "The bushes probably saved his life. But I don'na know how badly hurt he is. We should get him to a doctor right away."

Just then the boy groaned. The Palawanos broke out again in excited voices, a mixture of relief and anxiety.

Harry Edwards spoke to his foreman. "Tell them the boy needs a doctor. If they will let us, we will take him down the mountain and get help."

José spoke in Tagalog to the Palawanos spokesman, who translated for the others. Immediately an argument broke out. An old man, his wrinkled skin hanging loosely over his bones, pointed at the strangers and babbled wildly. The man with the necklace took it off and shook it in the old man's face, then talked excitedly to the tribal spokesman.

"The old man is the *panglima*—the village elder," Sandy Sutherland murmured. "I think he's trying to convince the others that this accident is our fault."

"But Mr. Edwards has been trading with them for years!" protested Alastair.

"Just pray, son. The lad needs help."

Finally the tribal spokesman turned to the trading party and rattled off many words in a mixture of Tagalog and Palawano. The porter then translated what he said into English. "The boy's name is Lastani. Lastani wanted his uncle to give him the family *lambos* charm to protect him from the evil spirits in the trees, but the uncle refused. The boy is supposed to wait two more rainy seasons before it passes to him. Now the uncle regrets being so stubborn. He says the boy would not have fallen out of the tree if he'd been wearing the necklace. The panglima doesn't want the boy to go, but the uncle gives his permission—but only if Lastani wears the lambos charm to protect him from more harm by the evil spirits."

Even as the foreman spoke, Alastair noticed the uncle carefully knotting the necklace around the injured boy's neck.

"We have no time to argue about 'evil spirits' here," murmured Mr. Edwards. His porters quickly went to work, cutting two strong poles from jungle saplings, then tying two empty canvas sacks to the poles to make a crude stretcher. The boy Lastani, groaning in pain, was gently picked up by several of the porters and laid on the stretcher, then strapped to the stretcher with strong vines. Four porters lifted the ends of the poles to their shoulders and followed Mr. Edwards down the mountain path.

The rest of the porters picked up the sacks of almaciga gum and fell into line. As Alastair and his father followed, Alastair noticed that four large sacks full of gum were still sitting on the ground. "Papa, look!" he said. "Mr. Edwards forgot some of his sacks."

Sandy Sutherland shook his head. "No, lad. He had to make a choice—take the gum or take Lastani."

❖ ❖ ❖

The Filipino doctor repacked his bag and closed it with a snap. "This is a lucky boy," he said to Maisie and Sandy Sutherland, who were standing at the foot of the boy's bed. "A clean break of the leg and two broken ribs—but that's all as far as I can tell. You say he fell from fifty feet up? Could've broken his neck! Speaking of his neck—this leather string is really too tight; he should breathe freely." The doctor started to remove the leather string, but with a sudden movement the boy fought off the doctor's hands, then cried out in pain.

"Better leave it alone," Sandy Sutherland sighed. "We promised the lad's uncle he could wear the necklace if we brought him down the mountain."

The trip down the mountain carrying Lastani had taken many hours, and night had fallen by the time they got back to Brooke's Point. Now it was well after midnight. The younger Sutherland children had fallen asleep in their parents' bed, but Alastair sat in the open window of the bedroom he shared with his little brothers, stroking Co-Co, his pet parrot, and watching as the doctor finished tending the injured boy. Lastani's eyes gradually closed, and his breathing became deeper as the sedative the doctor had given him took effect. Wide bandages bound his chest; his splinted leg was propped on a stack of pillows.

The doctor turned to go. "You mean well, Pastor Sutherland, but . . . if you ask my opinion, it was not wise to bring a tribal boy down from the mountain. Why, he cannot speak English—or even Tagalog. He is not used to a civilized town such as Brooke's Point—

much less a European household! What are you going to *do* with him while he is laid up for six weeks?"

"Well, he . . ." Maisie Sutherland looked at her husband, perplexed. Then her eyes brightened. "Why, he can go to school. School starts soon. I help teach some of the town children at the chapel. Alastair can help teach Lastani some English—and maybe Lastani can teach us some Palawano."

Alastair looked at his mother sharply. Lastani was going to *stay* with them? Giving up his bed for one night was one thing, but—six weeks? And when did he volunteer to become the older boy's nanny?

"We'll make up another bed for you, Alastair," his mother added hastily. "We really can'na put a boy with a broken leg on the floor."

The doctor shook his head. "Foolishness," he muttered as he walked out of the pleasant cottage into the warm tropical night.

❖ ❖ ❖ ❖

A few days later Alastair was helping his mother hang out wet sheets when he saw Harry Edwards coming into the yard with a pair of crutches. "Thought I'd stop by and see how the patient is doing," Mr. Edwards said jovially. He handed the crutches to Alastair. "Maybe you can show Lastani how to use these when he gets out of bed. Hey there, Sandy."

Hearing their American friend's voice, Sandy Sutherland had joined his wife and son out in the yard.

"Oh, wanted to let you folks know I sent off that

33

letter to Joy Ridderhof when the island steamer made its stop yesterday." Harry Edwards grinned sheepishly. "I know, I know—it's a long shot. But when Alastair found that article . . . well, I at least had to try. Can't just let Bertie's dream die."

"It's my dream, too," said Sandy Sutherland softly. "Having Lastani here, wearing that lambos charm . . . it's a constant reminder that his people live in fear of evil spirits and need the guid news of Jesus."

Within a few more days Lastani was hobbling about on the crutches, banging into things and sending Bao-Bao, Heather's pet kitten, scooting under the beds. Alastair didn't mind giving up his bed to the Palawanos boy so much—but it was frustrating living with someone he couldn't talk to. "I tried to tell Lastani not to pee in the garden," he complained to his mother, "but he just ignored me."

"Hmm, well . . . he's used to living outdoors," said Maisie Sutherland helplessly—and then she burst out laughing.

Alastair didn't think it was so funny. "But, Mama, he eats his rice and fish with his fingers and slurps rice porridge right from the bowl. And why won'na he sit at the table with us?"

"Be patient, son," she said, still chuckling. "He's a smart lad; he'll get the idea."

Though several years older than Alastair, Lastani was only a few inches taller. His skin was a rich golden brown, his thick black hair long and straight. His dark eyes darted here and there, taking in everything. But he said little, spending the first few days he was out of bed leaning on the crutches in the front yard of the Sutherlands' house, looking out at the Sulu Sea, chanting singsong words to himself.

But soon the older boy began following Alastair around and imitating the things he did. He made a face brushing his teeth with baking soda, but he gamely scrubbed away. He proudly pulled on the pair of shorts Maisie Sutherland made for him—*over* his bark loincloth. He stared when the family bowed their heads to say a blessing before each meal, but he politely bowed his head, too. Soon he was using a fork to spear vegetables and a spoon to shovel his rice. But when the saltshaker was passed to him, he shook the salt into his hand, looked at it blankly, then carefully tried to put it back through the little holes. The little boys giggled, but Lastani just laughed, too.

One of Alastair's weekly chores was weeding the large vegetable garden behind the Sutherland house. "If I'm going to have a shadow, might as well get some guid out of it," Alastair muttered, motioning Lastani to follow him. Lastani carefully watched as Alastair showed which plants to leave untouched and how to pull the weeds. Then, sitting on the ground with his splinted leg sticking out awkwardly, the older boy pulled weeds, too.

They had finished several rows in record time when Maisie Sutherland came out to the garden and pulled up a handful of carrots. The Palawanos boy followed her back to the house on his crutches and watched as she scrubbed them, boiled them, and served them for dinner.

"Carrots," she said.

"Keereets," he repeated.

She beamed at him. "I think it's time to start English lessons."

❖ ❖ ❖ ❖

Alastair pointed to the words on the piece of paper. "I . . . can . . . run . . . fast," he said, pointing to each word in turn as he said it. He pushed the paper to the older boy beside him. "Now you say it, Lastani."

The Palawanos boy repeated the words. "I . . . can . . . run . . . fast." He looked puzzled. "What mean?"

Alastair ran two of his fingers quickly over the bench the two boys were using as a desk, trying to imitate running. "Fingers? Dance?" Lastani asked.

Frustrated, Alastair shook his head. Why couldn't his mother help Lastani? But Mrs. Sutherland was reading to the youngest age group, and Mrs. Sola, the Filipino teacher, was helping Heather's age group with their numbers.

Alastair gazed out the window of the chapel that held the little Brooke's Point school. The monsoon rains that drenched the island daily had passed an hour earlier, leaving the dirt lanes and thatched roofs wet and steaming. He scowled. It was bad enough not being able to go to the boarding school in Manila for another year, but how was he going to learn anything *this* year if he spent all his time helping Lastani? It was already late August, and school had been in session for nearly three months. Lastani's broken leg and ribs had healed in good time, and he had given up the crutches several weeks ago. But when the doctor said he could go home now, Lastani had protested. *"No! No! Lastani stay school!"*

Alastair had to admit Lastani was a fast learner. Even the younger Sutherland children had made a game of pointing to various objects—chair, spoon, house, ladder, bucket, banana, palm tree—and saying the word in English. Lastani was soon repeating English words for almost everything. Verbs and whole sentences were harder, but once Lastani got the idea, he never forgot it. Alastair had to give him credit for that. But how long was Lastani going to stay?

The little bell that signaled the end of the school day interrupted Alastair's thoughts. Quickly he and Lastani gathered up their books and papers and made a beeline for the chapel door.

"Alastair, wait!" called his mother. With a sigh Alastair turned back as the other children pushed out the door, laughing and calling. "Would you and Lastani go to the market on your way home and pick up some fish for supper?" asked Maisie Sutherland. "Mrs. Sola and I are going to work on tomorrow's lesson plans. Heather will take Glen and Craigie home. But I saw the Moros fishermen coming to town today—there ought to be some guid mahimahi. Here, take my coin purse."

Alastair ran outside. "Lastani!" he called, waving

the coin purse. "Market!" This was one chore he didn't mind. The Brooke's Point market was always a noisy, exciting place. Men and women from the surrounding barrios, mostly along the coast, set up their food stalls loaded with everything from mangoes, pineapple, and cassava root to live chickens, goat meat, and fresh fish. Others sold handmade baskets, handwoven shawls, and jewelry made from shells and polished stones.

As the two boys skirted the puddles in the muddy lane, Alastair got an idea. He pointed to himself. "I!" he said. Then he jogged a little way down the lane. "Can run!" he shouted back at Lastani. Then he did it again, but this time running as fast as he could. "I can run . . . *fast!*"

Lastani laughed. "Yes! Yes! Run fast!" The Palawanos boy sprinted past Alastair with only a trace of a limp from the broken leg. "*I* can run fast!"

The two boys slowed to a walk as they turned into Market Street. The stalls were still being set up after the afternoon monsoon. They threaded their way through the crowded street and headed for the stalls of the Moros fishermen.

The Moros were Muslim tribesmen, known everywhere as excellent fishermen. Their stalls always had more variety of fish and shellfish than any of the other fish stalls. Alastair's father had once told him that there were eight different Muslim tribes in the Philippine Islands, but only a few of those lived on Palawan. Like Muslims everywhere, they carried their prayer mats and prayed toward Mecca five times a day.

Alastair and Lastani headed for a stall covered with bright red and yellow cloth, still dripping from the rain. A man with a blue turban sat on a wooden stool playing a wooden flute, surrounded by buckets of fresh fish. A long curved sword hung from his waist. Beside him, a tall boy about Lastani's age stood leaning against a *carabao* cart. His arms were folded, and his eyes were dark and brooding. He wore loose white pantaloons down to his ankles. An embroidered vest hung open on his bare chest, and a long knife with a jeweled handle hung at his side.

A shiver ran up and down Alastair's spine in spite of the hot, humid air. He was used to seeing the Moros men wearing the traditional curved sword or *kris*—or at least a serious-looking knife—strapped to their sides. But why was that boy looking at him and Lastani so strangely?

Alastair avoided the boy's eyes. "Mahimahi?" he asked the man.

The man stopped playing his flute, rose, and bowed his head politely. "How many?" he asked in English.

Alastair held up two fingers. The man dipped into a bucket and brought up two large, dripping fish. He quickly tied their tails together with a thin string of woven rattan and handed the end of the string to Alastair. The boy paid the man from his mother's coin purse and turned to go.

But where was Lastani?

Just then he heard Lastani's voice behind him. "Good knife! Lastani look?"

Quickly Alastair turned back to the stall. Lastani was admiring the Muslim boy's jewel-handled knife.

Slowly and deliberately the boy in the splendid clothes drew the knife from its sheath and laid it in Lastani's outstretched hands.

"Good knife!" Lastani said again admiringly.

The boy looked Lastani up and down. "Would you like a knife like this?" he said in careful English.

"Lastani, come on," Alastair said urgently. "We don't have money for a knife."

The stranger silenced Alastair with a swift, dark glance, then turned back to Lastani, standing with his legs apart and arms folded. "You are Palawanos, right? From the mountains?" He pointed at the steep expanse of rock and forest that towered above the town, then flashed an arrogant smile. "A brother Filipino!"

Lastani must have understood the gist of what the other boy was saying, because he nodded.

The Muslim boy pointed to the lambos charm that Lastani wore around his neck. "I see your people fear 'evil spirits.' But, my friend"—the tall boy leaned closer to Lastani's face—"you do not fear them enough!" He suddenly pointed at Alastair, then spit on the ground. "What in the name of Allah are you doing with this . . . this *Christian boy*?! I tell you: The only sure way to heaven is—"

The tall boy did not finish. But locking his eyes on Alastair, he took the knife from Lastani's hands, slowly put it back in its sheath, and with his other hand drew a finger across his throat.

Chapter 4

The Good-Luck Necklace

LASTANI SEEMED UNTROUBLED by the encounter with the boy in the market, but Alastair was upset. "He went like this, Papa!" he said that night at supper, drawing a finger across his throat.

"Sandy, do you think . . . ?" Maisie Sutherland asked uneasily.

"Nay, nay, he's just a lad," said her husband, deftly peeling the bony skeleton from the baked fish on the platter. "I know the father—a devout Muslim, but very polite. The lad's name is Ravi—a bit hot-blooded, but just talk."

Alastair resentfully watched Lastani noisily suck in a bite of the savory fish and smack his lips. "All Lastani cared about was the boy's fancy knife," he pouted.

Lastani's eyes lit up. "Good knife!" he said. "I want."

"A guid knife like that costs lots of money, Lastani," Alastair shot back. "Big money! And you don'na have any money."

Lastani looked confused, but Alastair turned back to his father. "But what did the Muslim boy mean by—"

Just then the screen door banged, and a man's voice called out, "Hello!"

"Harry!" said Sandy Sutherland, getting up from the table and greeting their guest. "Come and sit down. I'm afraid we've polished off the fish, but these bairns don't like dessert, so I'm sure there'll be plenty—"

The children greeted their father's teasing with a chorus of protest.

Harry Edwards laughed and pulled up an extra chair. "Don't worry, kids, I've already had my supper. But . . ." He pulled an envelope from his shirt pocket and waved it in the air. "A fishing boat brought mail, and guess who has written us a letter?"

"Mail?" said Maisie Sutherland. "How did mail come through during August monsoons—no! Not Miss Ridderhof!"

Harry Edwards was so excited, he could hardly sit in his chair. "Yes! Not only that—but she wrote to say that even before she got our letter, she was planning to leave for the Philippines in October of this very year!"

"She's *coming*?" shouted Sandy Sutherland. "Praise be to God! I was praying and hoping, but did'na really think—"

"Why, that's wonderful!" exclaimed Alastair's mother. "But that's less than two months away! And we still hav'na found anyone who can translate from English into Palawano."

"What about Lastani?" said Heather matter-of-factly. "If you hav'na noticed, he picks up English like Bao-Bao picks up fleas."

Everyone looked at the girl, and then at Lastani. Alastair rolled his eyes. What did his sister know about it?

Mr. Edwards stroked his chin. "Heather, you may be on to something—"

"But . . . October?" protested Maisie Sutherland. "It's almost September now. I mean, Lastani *is* learning fast, but he does'na know English well enough yet to translate."

"True, true," said Harry Edwards. "But October is just when Miss Ridderhof's ship leaves Los Angeles. Here, listen . . ." He scanned through the letter again. "She's going to record several languages on Luzon and some of the other islands first. She says to let her know if we can make the arrangements on our end, and she'll try to come to Palawan as well." He looked up. "My guess is it will be another five or six months."

"I see," Maisie Sutherland said thoughtfully. "In six months, Lastani just might be able to—"

Sandy Sutherland held up his hands. "Everyone

just hold on . . . hold on here," he said. "Harry, I'm as eager as you are to get the Gospel recorded into Palawano. This is a wonderful opportunity! But"— the pastor's eyes rested on Lastani, who was looking from one adult to the other with a puzzled look—"we can'na keep Lastani indefinitely. His leg has healed almost completely, and, frankly, it's time to take him home."

"You're right, Sandy!" Harry Edwards agreed, slapping the table. "I've been thinking about Lastani, too. We've all noticed what a bright boy he is, and he's already learned so much English. I've also noticed that he seems to like working in your garden, Maisie. He has a good eye for growing things. Why not—" Mr. Edwards' eyes danced. "Why not send Lastani to the Farm School in Aborlan next year? I'm prepared to pay his tuition. Why, the things he would learn there could be very useful to his barrio in the mountains—and all the Palawanos tribespeople, for that matter!"

"But, Harry!" protested Sandy Sutherland. "We can'na just—"

"No, no, of course we can't just do it! We'll take him back to his barrio and ask his family's permission to let him come back here to finish the school year, then go to the Farm School next June."

"Well," said Sandy Sutherland thoughtfully, "I suppose if he had his family's permission to continue to study . . . it *would* be wonderful if he could translate for Miss Ridderhof whenever she comes to Brooke's Point."

"Somebody better ask Lastani what *he* wants to do," Alastair grumbled. It was wonderful, of course, to hear that the Ridderhof lady might be able to come to Palawan Island and make recordings in the Palawan language. But Alastair's feelings were still raw from the Moros boy's threats at the market, and nobody else seemed to even care. And if he had to help tutor Lastani for the whole rest of the year, he might never be ready to go to boarding school next June!

"Out of the mouths of the children!" laughed Harry Edwards. "Maisie and Sandy, your kids have more wisdom than the lot of us put together. Lastani"—he turned to the dark-haired boy, who still had a puzzled look on his face—"would you like to stay here and continue to go to school?"

"Yes. I stay. Go school," said Lastani.

"Hmm, Maisie, help me," said Harry Edwards helplessly. "How do we explain about the Farm School, and about helping to translate Bible records into Palawano?"

Slowly and patiently, Maisie Sutherland tried to explain about going to a school in Aborlan, seventy miles up the coast, after the next dry season to learn how to grow food.

Again Lastani said quickly, "Yes. I go Farm School."

Sandy Sutherland took over. "Lastani, a woman is coming—here—to tell the Jesus story. The same Jesus story I talk about on Sunday at the chapel." Lastani gave a slow nod. "She is going to put the

Jesus story in a . . . a . . . how should I say 'record player'? A talking box! A box that talks in Lastani's ain language. When you learn more English, you could help her."

The boy frowned. "Talking box? No, no. Lastani not help." He clutched the lambos charm around his neck.

Alastair saw his parents look at each other helplessly. How could they help Lastani understand the difference between an "evil spirit" and a tape recorder? As they tried to explain that a "talking box" was just a machine, Alastair idly picked up the letter from Joy Ridderhof that Mr. Edwards had laid on the table. A phrase at the bottom of the page caught his eye.

"Hey," he said suddenly. "Miss Ridderhof says she will pay the translator for help." He looked at Lastani. "Pay *money*."

"Money?" Lastani's eyes lit up. "Money for good knife?" A wide grin spread across his face. "Yes. Lastani help."

✧ ✧ ✧ ✧

The monsoons continued to lash the east coast of Palawan well into September before it was safe to travel into the mountains. Mr. Edwards could not go; there would not be any almaciga gum for trade so soon after monsoon season, and he and his workers were busy harvesting coconuts. So it was decided that Sandy Sutherland and Alastair would go with Lastani back up the mountain trail to Lastani's village—or as close as they would be allowed to go with him.

The night before they left, Alastair went into the sitting room to cover Co-Co's cage for the night and heard his parents talking as they sat out in the yard, catching the gentle night breeze coming up from the beach.

"I'm going to miss Lastani," his mother said wistfully.

"He'll be back," his father encouraged.

"Yes . . . but what if his family won'na give their permission for him to come back? We may have missed our golden opportunity to bring him to Jesus."

"Nay, nay, Maisie, we mus'na think like that," replied Sandy Sutherland. "We have planted and watered many seeds. It's up to the Holy Ghost to grow them up. All in God's ain guid time."

Alastair's mother sighed. "I know. But . . . he still lives in fear of evil spirits. I tried to tell him the power of Jesus is greater than the evil spirits, but he just smiled and said that he liked Jesus *and* his lambos charm."

Might as well add Allah to Lastani's religious stew, Alastair thought as he covered the bird's cage. He wondered if his parents knew how often Lastani went to the market to talk to the Moros boy about buying the fine knife. Alastair had no doubt Ravi was trying to convince "brother Lastani" that "there is no God but Allah."

But even Ravi could not make Lastani take off the lambos charm. Just two days earlier Alastair and Lastani had run into Ravi at the market, even though Alastair tried to avoid the fish stall. As usual, Ravi had ignored Alastair and asked if he could see the necklace that Lastani wore snugly around his neck.

Lastani had jerked back. *"No! No touch!"*

"Why?" Ravi had insisted. *"You wear it so tight. It looks uncomfortable."*

"Lambos like . . . like skin. Lambos warn danger, get tight, like so—" Lastani had squeezed Ravi's arm.

❖ ❖ ❖ ❖

The next morning Sandy Sutherland led the way up the first half of the trail, but as the trail grew steeper and more hidden beneath the ferns, Lastani took the lead. Alastair, bringing up the rear, suddenly realized the tables had turned. Back in Brooke's Point, Lastani was the "stranger," the one who needed to be taught what to do. But here in the forest, Lastani knew its secrets, and Alastair and his father were the strangers and intruders.

As Alastair pulled himself up the mountain trail, using tree roots and sharp pieces of stone to give himself a boost, he wondered about what Lastani had said the other day. The lambos charm couldn't *really* warn him about danger, could it? Wasn't all that stuff about evil spirits just superstition?

Alastair felt sweat running down his face. It was so humid in the forest after the monsoons! He really needed a drink. Rubbing the back of his hand across

his forehead, he called out, "Wait, Lastani! Can'na we stop—"

"Hsssssh!" Lastani made a sudden hushing sound and held up his hand for quiet. Alastair saw him grip the lambos charm and hold perfectly still for a few minutes. Both Alastair and his father obediently stood still. Alastair listened, but he couldn't hear anything unusual. Even the treetops were quiet, except for the chattering and trilling of birds and water dripping from the palm fronds onto the lush ferns and tall grasses below.

Again Lastani motioned for silence, but he began moving again up the steep path, slower now, looking this way and that. Alastair felt impatient. Was Lastani showing off? Trying to make them feel like there was some danger in the forest? He really wanted to stop and take a drink from the canteen his father wore—

"Down!" yelled Lastani, and in the same moment Alastair saw—no, felt—Lastani throw himself at Sandy Sutherland, who reached out an arm and pulled Alastair down with him as the three bodies tumbled off the path and into the thick undergrowth.

Alastair's face nose-dived into the dirt, and his father's stocky body landed across him, pinning him. He jerked his face to the side, spitting out dirt, twigs, and leaves so he could breathe. "Aggh!" he spluttered, but again he heard Lastani hiss, "Hssssh."

The three of them lay silently in the brush for several long minutes before Lastani finally scrambled to his feet. Sandy Sutherland rolled off Alastair and helped his son stand up.

"Lastani?" said Sandy Sutherland quietly. "What happened?"

But Lastani was looking carefully in the brush just beyond where they had fallen. Alastair rolled his eyes. If Lastani was playing some stupid game with them, trying to impress them, he for one was going to—

"Ah!" Lastani exclaimed suddenly and pulled something from the trunk of a tree. He held it up for the ruddy-faced father and son to see: a small, straight arrow with a very sharp point.

"A blowgun dart!" exclaimed Sandy Sutherland. "Do you mean someone—"

"Yes," Lastani nodded soberly. "Someone try kill."

"But . . . but how did you know?" Alastair's father asked.

Lastani's hand went to the piece of carved bone tied snugly around his neck. "The lambos charm warn danger." He smiled broadly. "Very good luck, yes?"

Chapter 5

Dashed Hopes

ALASTAIR WAS SPEECHLESS. Someone in the forest had tried to kill them—and Lastani had saved them! He looked around fearfully. Were they still . . . ?

As if reading their minds, Lastani said, "Not worry. Gone away." Then to Alastair's amazement, he unbuttoned his shirt and peeled off the khaki shorts Maisie had made for him. He melted into the bushes and in a few moments came back wearing only a thin vine around his waist and soft, broad leaves made into a loincloth. "Friends go home," he said. "Lastani go barrio alone."

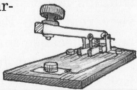

"But . . . Lastani," said Sandy Sutherland. "We want to ask your family about coming back with us—to learn English and go to the Farm School!"

"Lastani ask. Lastani come back." He gave them a reassuring grin and a wave, tucked the shirt and shorts under his arm, then disappeared into the dense undergrowth of graceful ferns and wide elephant leaves.

Father and son listened, but they heard nothing except the *drip, drip* from the trees and the occasional screech of a parrot.

Sandy Sutherland shrugged. "I guess we go home, lad. Lastani probably felt safer going the rest of the way without us."

Alastair was only too glad to fall in step behind his father on the narrow trail as they descended the mountain. "But, Papa," he said, "who tried to kill us with the blowgun? It was'na Lastani's people, was it?"

"I don'na think so, lad," said his father. "Maybe a scout for another tribe who did'na recognize Lastani as Palawanos with town clothes on. And we had no goods to trade . . . so maybe they were trying to scare us off."

Alastair tried to keep his footing on the damp, slick path. "But, Papa, Lastani's lambos charm did'na really warn him about the danger, did it? I mean, that's all just superstition, isn't it?"

"Some of their beliefs are just superstition, yes," said his father. "But Satan and his evil spirits are very real. The Palawanos give them even more power, because they fear them and don't know the guid news about Jesus, who broke the power of the Evil One. But as for the lambos charm . . ." Sandy

Sutherland fell quiet for a long time. Alastair was going to ask him again, when his father said, "I can'na say what happened, lad. But I don'na believe in 'guid luck.' We must thank our heavenly Father for sparing our lives."

❖ ❖ ❖ ❖

One week went by . . . then two, then three, and still no sign of Lastani. "When is Lastani coming back?" whimpered Craigie one night at bedtime as the Sutherlands gathered for family prayers. The little boy had gotten used to having another big brother.

"Maybe he got killed by the man with the blowgun," offered Glen helpfully.

"Stop it, Glen!" snapped Alastair. "Lastani's too smart to get himself killed. He saved Papa and me, remember?" Alastair was surprised at how much he missed the Palawanos boy. Sure, it was nice having his own bed back . . . but somehow the days seemed longer and emptier without Lastani and his good-natured determination to learn English and try new ways.

"Why did'na his family let him come back?" Heather wondered sadly.

"Well, we don'na know that he won'na come back. But I imagine his family was verra glad to see him and wanted to keep him awhile." Maisie Sutherland tried to sound cheerful.

"Ay. Maybe we were selfish to want him to come back," Sandy Sutherland admitted. "But . . . God knows Joy Ridderhof is on her way to the Philippines and that we need a translator to do the gospel records. We must pray and leave the whole matter in our heavenly Father's hands."

Alastair heard the hint of disappointment in his parents' voices. He felt a little mad at Lastani for not coming back . . . and mad at God, too, for raising his parents' hopes—and Mr. Edwards' hopes—about the gospel records.

The next day in school, Alastair had just finished reciting the principal rivers in Africa and had taken his seat when he glanced out the window. A familiar figure in a rumpled white shirt and khaki shorts was striding up the lane.

"Lastani!" he cried.

Immediately all the school children rushed for the windows. "Lastani! Apo! Hello!" they cried. Glen and Craigie and the other young ones hopped up and down excitedly.

Alastair couldn't help grinning as the mountain boy walked into the chapel school, his long dark hair bound up on the side, Palawanos fashion. "I come back," he said simply.

That evening, the Sutherland household invited Mr. and Mrs. Edwards to a "welcome back" supper for Lastani. It was a noisy celebration, with everyone trying to talk at once. Finally, when everyone had had their fill of savory goat stew and *ginatan*, a sweet dessert of yam, sweet potato, and bananas in coconut milk, Sandy Sutherland pushed back his plate.

"I think I'll walk down to the telegraph office," he

said with a sly grin. "Anyone want to go along?"

Everyone wanted to go along. The adults walked along the soft, warm sand of the beach toward the town, while the children raced at the edge of the water, squealing as the lip of the tide rushed in and wet their feet. At the telegraph office—combination weather station, shipping office, and post office—the Filipino attendant asked to whom the telegram should be sent.

"To Joy Ridderhof," said Sandy Sutherland. "In care of the Far East Broadcasting Company, Manila."

"Message?" said the attendant, licking the tip of his pencil. The Scottish pastor handed him a slip of paper. The attendant read it aloud:

WELCOME STOP LARGE OPPORTUNITY
FOR RECORDS HERE STOP
    Signed: Pastor Sandy Sutherland
    Brooke's Point, Palawan

❖ ❖ ❖ ❖

Lastani's English improved remarkably in the weeks and months that followed his return to Brooke's Point. He was an eager student, always asking questions, never shy to admit he didn't know something. By the time Alastair turned twelve, Lastani had worked his way through the first, second, and third grade English reader and began learning Filipino. English and Filipino were both "official" languages in the Philippines.

"The boy has a gift," said Mr. Edwards admiringly, hearing Lastani read one evening at the

Sutherland home. "Once he completes two years at the Farm School, we should maybe think about a college education."

"Slow down, Harry!" laughed Sandy Sutherland. "One thing at a time."

Harry Edwards grinned. "Hey, an export businessman has to think big. And a Christian missionary has to think even bigger," he teased.

Alastair, slouched behind his sixth grade mathematics book doing his homework, perked up his ears. He liked Mr. Edwards' gung-ho approach to everything. Alastair hadn't told anyone yet, but he sometimes thought about being a Christian businessman like Mr. Edwards. Not on Palawan Island, but maybe somewhere else in the Philippines . . . or maybe Australia . . . or, why not Africa or South America? His papa always said Mr. Edwards was kind of like a missionary, too—concerned about the welfare of his workers and the people in the area, and a faithful supporter of the local church.

"It's already January," said Sandy Sutherland, interrupting Alastair's thoughts. "Do we know when she's coming?"

Everyone knew who "she" was. Joy Ridderhof.

Harry Edwards shook his head. "I've been meeting every island steamer—they're running pretty regularly now that the rainy season is past. But no passengers."

"That's all right," said Maisie Sutherland. "We can use the time. Lastani is helping me translate some gospel choruses into Palawano," she laughed.

"I tell him the word or phrase in English, he says something in Palawano, and I write down what the words *sound* like. Miss Ridderhof's letter said they like to include Christian songs if they can. Some of the school girls volunteered to sing, but we still need time to practice."

"Ay, there are still several months before Lastani has to leave for school," agreed Alastair's father.

"Me too, don'na forget," piped up Alastair. Sometimes he felt as if no one remembered that he was going away to boarding school in June. His parents, the Edwardses, the members of Brooke's Point Chapel, the chapel school—everyone was excited about the arrival of Joy Ridderhof.

Lastani was excited about the recording project, too—but for a different reason. At least once a week the Palawanos boy went to the market to admire Ravi's knife. The Moros boy still ignored Alastair, but he had not made any other threats, so Alastair usually tagged along. One day Lastani got bold and said, "I would like to buy your knife."

Ravi raised his eyebrows. "Your English is very good, Lastani. But my knife is not for sale." Seeing Lastani's disappointment, the Muslim boy hastened to add, "Perhaps I can get one like it for you. But . . . do you have money?"

Lastani shook his head. "No. I have not the money now. But I will soon." He drew himself up proudly. "I am going to—how do you say it?—put English words into Palawano for American woman."

"*American* woman?" said Ravi, his eyes narrowing. "There is no American woman in Brooke's Point."

"But Joy woman is coming," said Lastani stubbornly. "She will pay money. Please, find good knife with fine handle. I want to buy."

The moderate weather months of January, February, and March 1950 passed, and gradually the temperature began to rise. School break arrived in April—and still Miss Ridderhof had not arrived. Every time an island steamer tooted its whistle and anchored offshore, the children scampered to the beach to see if a *boaty*—a small dinghy with a gas motor—would bring back a passenger. But it was only the mail, bags of rice, and trade goods for Mr. Edwards.

During the school break, Mr. Edwards took Lastani with him on some of his trading trips into the mountains to practice translating from English directly into Palawano. "He's wonderful!" Mr. Edwards reported enthusiastically after Lastani's first trip. "No middleman, no loss of meaning going from English to Tagalog to Palawano... The Palawanos seem very proud of him. I told you this boy could open the door to wonderful new things for the Palawanos tribes!"

But as the weeks passed, they did not hear from Miss Ridderhof, and the Edwardses and Sutherlands met to face the unthinkable: Miss Ridderhof might not come.

"I don't understand it," said Mr. Edwards. Disappointment was etched in his face. "She seemed very willing to put Palawan into her schedule while she was here in the Philippines."

"It's more than six months since she arrived in Manila," said Sandy Sutherland. "Maybe she had to return to Los Angeles and did not know how to contact us."

"A letter may yet come, explaining," said Maisie gently. "You know how slow the mail is in the islands."

Mr. Edwards sighed. "If she is not on the next steamer . . . we must send Lastani. Otherwise he will not arrive in time for the beginning of the Farm School."

Sandy Sutherland nodded. "Yes. Alastair too. I plan to go with both boys and take Alastair all the way to Manila and get him settled in the boarding school."

Alastair had a headache. He had had one all day. But listening to his father, his heart skipped a beat. He was sorry about the recording project, but he couldn't help feeling excited about a trip by steamer five hundred miles to Manila. It would be fun traveling with Lastani the first couple of days. At boarding school he would meet lots of new friends—Filipino, American, English, African . . . children of missionaries, diplomats, government officials, and business people. And *finally* he would get a chance to play basketball!

Lastani's voice broke into Alastair's thoughts. "You say the Joy woman is not coming?" the Palawanos boy asked curtly.

Mr. Edwards shrugged helplessly. "We . . . don't

know, Lastani. But the next boat must take you and Alastair to school."

"We are verra, verra sorry, Lastani," said Maisie Sutherland gently.

The Palawanos boy said nothing but turned and walked stiffly out of the house, heading for the town.

"Go with him, lad," Sandy Sutherland said to Alastair.

"But, Papa, I have a headache—"

"Go now, lad. Lastani needs a friend right now."

Alastair sighed and let the screen door slam behind him. He didn't feel like rushing after Lastani, who was already halfway down the lane toward town. But he followed, trying to keep Lastani in sight so he could catch up to him. When Lastani turned into Market Street, Alastair muttered, "Should have known."

The market stalls were being taken down and food and handcrafts reloaded into carabao carts or large gunnysacks. Sure enough, Lastani was talking to Ravi as the Moros boy loaded the fish buckets onto the family's carabao cart.

The two older boys did not see Alastair as he came closer and stood behind the next stall. "What do you mean you cannot buy the knife!" Ravi demanded. "I bought one from my uncle's friend who makes knives to sell to you. If you do not buy, I will lose my money!"

"I am sorry much," pleaded Lastani. "I want to buy, but . . . American woman has not come. And now I must go to Farm School. I leave on next boat."

"Huh!" snorted Ravi, banging the fish buckets into the cart. "There never was an American woman. It is all a lie!" He whirled on Lastani. "Now you know. The white Christians—they are just using you. They never intended to pay you any money. That was just fish bait to get you to go to school and learn English. Then they will use you to exploit the Palawanos people!"

"Exploit?" said Lastani in a puzzled voice.

Alastair wished he could sit down. His head hurt, and he felt both hot and cold at the same time. What in the world was Ravi talking about? It wasn't a lie. It just didn't happen.

"Yes, exploit! Talk sweet to the Palawanos to get the almaciga gum, labor, whatever they want. But they will not pay."

"But . . . what about Farm School? I should not go?" said Lastani.

Ravi laughed harshly. Then he lowered his voice. Alastair had to strain to hear. "No, let the American pay for the Farm School. You will learn much to benefit your people. But do not swallow their Christian God. Pretend to believe it; then, when you are finished, denounce the infidels. Go back to your people. Use what you have learned to help your tribe—not the Christian liars."

Alastair wanted to go home. He wanted a drink of water. He would talk to Lastani later, tell him it wasn't true . . . what Ravi said. Alastair turned to go, but he felt dizzy. He tripped over a bundle of bamboo poles and sprawled on the ground. Then he heard

Lastani's voice. It sounded close and far away at the same time.

"Alastair? . . . Alastair! . . . Why are you lying on the ground? . . . He's burning up, Ravi! Very bad fever. Here . . . help me get him up—uh! I must take him home."

❖ ❖ ❖ ❖

Alastair lay in his bed, teeth chattering, hair and clothes damp against his skin, as the Filipino doctor examined him. The doctor straightened up. "Malaria," he said crisply. "All the symptoms—chills, fever, sweating. I'll test this blood sample to be sure, but—"

"Malaria!" said Alastair's mother. "But . . . he's supposed to leave on the next steamer for boarding school!"

"Not this time," said the doctor dryly, shaking his head. "The fever will return every two or three days for a while. Then he will need to rest for several weeks. Give him these tablets each day—a new medicine, supposed to be better than quinine."

Alastair closed his eyes and groaned. No! It wasn't fair! Not go to school? If he didn't go now, he'd have to wait another whole year!

Chapter 6

A Dream Come True?

AWK! AWK!" SQUAWKED THE COCKATOO, rattling his cage with his beak.

Alastair looked up from the book he was reading. "Oh, all right, Co-Co," he sighed. "I want out of this cage, too." He dumped Heather's cat off his lap and stood up. It was Saturday morning, but the house was quiet and empty. Only the sounds of a stiff offshore breeze rattled in the coconut palms outside. Alastair's mother, sister, and little brothers had gone to take food to a family whose mother was sick. His father had gone off to talk to Harry Edwards, who had taken advantage of the break in the weather for a trading trip into the mountains the day before. He had brought back one of the men from Lastani's tribe.

Alastair opened Co-Co's cage door and let the little gray bird run up his arm to his shoulder. He slipped a small red cord over one of Co-Co's feet and tied the other end to his belt so the parrot couldn't fly away. Then he stepped outside. The palm trees waved against a blue and cloudless sky, which wouldn't have been strange if it were January or April, but it was August, usually one of the worst months of the monsoon season, and it hadn't rained since last week.

Alastair hesitated. He was supposed to be doing his schoolwork, trying to keep up with his class. But he was so *bored* being cooped up in the house since his bout with malaria! He hadn't had any fever for several weeks now, and he felt fine. But his mother was worried that he'd have a relapse if he got over tired. Still, a walk on the beach with Co-Co would keep him from going nuts. It was Saturday, after all!

The tide was in, and Alastair let the foamy surf wash over his bare feet. He wondered how Lastani was doing at the Farm School— No, he wasn't going to think about Lastani, or the girls who had gone off to school in Puerto Princesa. Everybody his age or older had gone off to school—everybody except him. Alastair felt the familiar surge of anger and disappointment.

But he had to admit, he wasn't the only one who was disappointed. Lastani was disappointed because he didn't get to translate for the American woman and earn money for the jewel-handled knife. His parents and Mr. Edwards were disappointed because Miss Ridderhof didn't come, and now there would be no gospel records for the Palawanos after all. Except . . . Alastair shook his head. He didn't understand Mr. Edwards. When he had come back from the mountains yesterday, he had brought back the Palawanos spokesman, the one who understood Tagalog.

"What are you thinking, man?" Sandy Sutherland had asked his friend when Mr. Edwards dropped by the house in the late evening.

Harry Edwards grinned and shrugged in the boyish way he had. *"Well, I was thinking, just in case Miss Ridderhof might still come, we ought to have someone who can translate into Palawano. So I found out his name, Primo, and—"*

"But the man can'na understand English!" said Alastair's father.

"True. True. But my foreman speaks both English and Tagalog, and Primo speaks a little Tagalog and Palawano, so . . . well, it will take some doing, but we might still get something translated. Thought we could try it out; then if the time comes . . ." He had smiled again. *"Can't let Bertie's dream die."*

Alastair sank down on the warm white sand in the shade of some coconut trees that leaned out over the beach. Bertie's dream . . . Why didn't they just admit it? God had let them all down! Nothing had happened like it was supposed to.

"Ouch," he said, slapping at Co-Co, who was nibbling his ear. Alastair leaned back against the scaly trunk of a tree and closed his eyes. He liked hearing the surf rolling in and the *screee, screee* of the sea gulls—

Alastair's eyes flew open. There was another sound . . . there it was again! The long, drawn-out hoot of an interisland steamer's whistle.

Alastair shaded his eyes against the glare of the morning sun. The usual number of *vintas* were out—the outrigger fishing canoes with their colorful square sails. Then he saw it: the single smokestack of a steamer, chugging around the bend into Brooke's Point Bay.

The interisland steamers had no fixed schedule in the monsoon months. They sailed when there was a break in the weather. In fact, during August Brooke's Point was usually pretty isolated because of the rough storms. A thought sprouted at the back of Alastair's brain: *If the ships are running, why can'na I go to school?*

The thought prodded Alastair to his feet, and he headed down the beach toward the town. Already he could see that the arrival of the steamer had created a beehive of activity on shore. Mr. Edwards' men were shouting to one another and working fast, loading the gunnysacks of almaciga gum onto a bevy of small rafts and boats. Working right alongside them, standing a head taller than most of the Filipinos, was Mr. Edwards. Off to the side, watching somewhat anxiously, stood Primo, the Palawanos man, wearing an open shirt and a bark loincloth. Alastair recognized him as the one who had greeted them on the trail when he had gone up the mountain with his father and Mr. Edwards the year before.

The steamer had dropped anchor out in deep water. Squinting against the sun, Alastair could just barely make out the name of the small ship: *Fortuna II*. The deck was crowded with passengers taking the opportunity to go from one island or town to another. A boaty headed out toward the steamer to pick up the mail and any passengers who might want to come ashore.

Alastair felt a hand on his shoulder. He looked up into his father's face. "I see you and Co-Co escaped the house, eh, lad?" Sandy Sutherland smiled.

"Papa, if the ships are running, why can'na I go to school?" Alastair blurted. "The school said I could come late once I got well."

"I know, I know, lad," said his father. "But neither your mither nor I can take you to Manila now. The monsoons might come any day, and then we would'na be able to get back."

"But, Papa—"

"Besides, I have a trip scheduled to visit the barrios along the coast next week. . . . Nay, lad. You'll just have to wait till next school year now."

Alastair kicked viciously at the sand. Co-Co squawked at the sudden movement. It just wasn't fair!

"What's this?" he heard his father suddenly exclaim. Alastair looked up. Out in the bay, two small figures were climbing down the rope ladder over the side of the steamer to the boaty pulled alongside. They didn't look like sailors. They didn't have black hair like Filipinos. . . .

"It's two women," said Sandy Sutherland in astonishment. "Foreigners . . ." Suddenly the missionary pastor began yelling and pointing. "Harry! Harry Edwards! Look! They've come! They've come!"

❖ ❖ ❖ ❖

"*Babai! Babai!*" "Women! Women!" Word spread rapidly through Brooke's Point that the American ladies from Gospel Recordings had arrived.

Alastair would never forget his first impression as the boaty stopped several yards from shore. The boatmen leaped knee deep into the water, lifted their passengers over the side, and deposited them, laughing, onto dry land. Both women were middle-aged, dressed in plain cotton blouses, seersucker skirts, and sandals. Ann Sherwood was the taller of the two, with plain brown hair, warm eyes behind her glasses, and a quiet smile. Joy Ridderhof's hair was a halo of silvery gray, and she wore a radiant smile as if her name—"Joy"—was written all over her suntanned face.

"Here at last!" boomed Sandy Sutherland, grinning from ear to ear. The next hour was a flurry of introductions, and sending Alastair off to find his mother, and hunting up a carabao cart to bring the luggage. But no sooner did their visitors arrive at the Sutherland house than a steady stream of towns-

people began dropping in to welcome them. Joy Ridderhof and her teammate, Ann Sherwood, seemed a little startled that everyone seemed to know about the recording project.

"We have never been so . . . so *expected* before!" they laughed.

Alastair could hardly believe Joy Ridderhof was actually sitting at their table. It seemed like a dream—Bertie's dream—come true. He watched Miss Ridderhof and Miss Sherwood as they talked and laughed and hungrily bit into the rice cakes and sweet slices of mangoes that Maisie Sutherland served for lunch. Little Craigie stood between the two women, looking in awe from one to the other.

"And what are you looking at, young man?" teased Miss Ridderhof.

Maisie Sutherland gave a little laugh. "Please don'na mind Glen and Craigie. Neither one has ever seen a white woman before, other than me. In fact, we hav'na had any foreign visitors here in Brooke's Point since the war."

"Never? But what about Mrs. Edwards?" asked Joy Ridderhof. "Mr. Edwards is American, isn't he?"

"She's Filipino," said Heather in a superior, don't-you-know-anything tone.

"Speaking of Edwards," said Sandy Sutherland, "here's Harry now with the carabao cart and all your luggage."

Alastair and his father helped unload the carabao cart and bring the various suitcases and bags into the house. "I know it seems like a lot," said Miss Ridderhof sheepishly, "but it's nothing compared to the equipment we used to lug around when we had to bring along our own generator. Now we have *this*." Beaming, she held up a red leather case, about sixteen inches long and six inches tall. "This is the 'Minadyk'—our new battery-powered recording machine."

Immediately the conversation turned to the reason for their visit—recording gospel messages in the Palawano language. "If it's all right with Sandy," said Harry Edwards, "I thought we could begin recording this evening over in the chapel—it'll be quieter there. Besides, I need a little time to get my translators together." He grinned. "We just happen to have a Palawanos tribesman with us for a few days—even though we didn't know you'd be coming today."

" 'Just happen to,' nothing!" laughed Joy Ridderhof. "Isn't that just how God works? We do our part, you do your part—and God puts it all together!"

"Well, this evening, then," said Maisie Sutherland, standing up and starting to clear the dishes from the table. "That will give me time to get our little trio together and run over some of the songs we've been practicing."

"You've been practicing *music* in Palawano already?" said Miss Sherwood. She turned to her companion. "Joy, these dear people are so prepared. I just know *this* recording session is going to go smooth as silk."

"We had some trouble with the Minadyk recorder at our last recording session in Puerto Princesa," Joy Ridderhof explained. "But we had it repaired just before we came, and it's working perfectly now."

"God is so guid!" beamed Sandy Sutherland. "Now—children, why don'na you take Miss Ridderhof and Miss Sherwood for a nice walk along the beach while we set things up for recording tonight."

"Oh, lovely!" said Miss Ridderhof.

Squealing, Heather, Glen, and Craigie dashed out the door. Alastair quickly put Co-Co back in his cage and started to follow. "Alastair, I'm sorry," said his mother, "but you can'na go. Papa says you already walked the beach into town this morning. That's enough exercise for one day." She turned apologetically to the two women. "Alastair had a recent bout of malaria and is still recovering."

"But, Mama!" protested Alastair. "I'm perfectly fine! I—"

Joy Ridderhof laid a gentle hand on his arm. "I'm sure resting is hard for an active boy like you," she said sympathetically. "But let me tell you a secret: The hard things in life are 'good rejoicing practice.' That's the way we overcome the difficulties Satan puts in our path. Rejoice about everything!"

From a window Alastair watched the beach party disappear around the bend that headed away from town. "Rejoice?" he muttered. "I never heard anything so stupid!"

Chapter 7

"Good Rejoicing Practice"

"Mama, please!" Alastair whispered, pulling his mother over near Co-Co's cage. "How many times do I have to tell you? I . . . feel . . . *fine!*"

The sun had slipped behind the rugged mountains flanking the town even before the beachcombers returned, and now the evening shadows sent long fingers out into the restless Sulu Sea. Ann Sherwood had already gone with Alastair's father to the chapel to set up the recording machine. His mother and Joy Ridderhof were planning to meet Harry Edwards with his two translators at the chapel shortly.

"But if you stayed home, then I could leave the little ones so they would'na bother the recording session," said his mother quietly.

"I don't mean to interfere," Joy Ridderhof said cheerfully from the table where she was finishing a cup of tea, "but we really don't mind if *all* the children come." She chuckled. "We often end up recording on the porch of a bamboo hut, with the usual number of pigs and chickens grunting and squawking underneath!"

Maisie Sutherland couldn't help but laugh. "Oh, all right. Come on, everyone, let's go—but you must *all* be quiet during the recording."

As the Sutherland children led the way past the coconut groves, then up the lane toward the chapel, Joy Ridderhof exclaimed over the neat rows of bamboo homes on stilts and colorful bougainvillea bushes. "Brooke's Point is truly a paradise!"

"August isn't usually like this," warned Maisie Sutherland. "Palawan Island is usually drowning in monsoons at this time of year."

Miss Ridderhof's eyes twinkled. "All the more reason to rejoice! God held back the rains so we could come."

Alastair could hear the schoolgirls singing as they drew near to the chapel. Were they recording already? But as they entered the chapel door, he saw Miss Sherwood sitting on a bench, with the Minadyk recorder opened up and various parts lying on another bench in front of her.

Joy Ridderhof gave a little start. "Is something wrong, Ann?"

"Oh!" Her partner shrugged. "It's just that—well,

I can't believe I'm not just forgetting to do some simple little thing, but so far the machine acts dead."

"Dead!" chorused Glen and Craigie in horror.

"Now, now, don't worry," said Miss Ridderhof. "We usually have a test like this to begin with, but it *always* works eventually. Let's just keep rejoicing in what God is going to do." She looked around. "I'm sure we can use the time practicing the scripts with our translators. Where is Mr. Edwards and—oh, there they are."

Harry Edwards was sitting with José, his foreman, and Primo, the Palawanos man. José was reading from an English script, one sentence at a time, and translating it aloud into Tagalog. Primo, listening, would then say it aloud in Palawano.

The tall American's tan face flashed a broad smile as Joy Ridderhof joined them. "I can hardly believe this day has come," he said. "This is the dream of my boy come true!"

"Your boy?" Miss Ridderhof said, puzzled.

Mr. Edwards chuckled. "Ah! You haven't heard our story." Alastair sprawled on a bench and listened as Mr. Edwards told the story of Bertie returning from college in America with a crazy idea—making gospel records in the language of primitive tribes who had no written language. He told about their two families hiding in the jungle during the war, with no proper medical care, and how Bertie's dream was one of the last things he talked about before he died of blackwater fever. "We talked often of Bertie's dream but had no idea how to make it happen. That is, until Alastair, here, found that article about your work in the *Sunday School Times*. We felt sure you could help us, but"—Mr. Edwards' grin broadened— "we didn't think that you yourself would come!"

Joy Ridderhof seemed very moved. "What a wonderful testimony to God's faithfulness," she murmured.

Several of the older girls who had practiced the Palawano songs had gone away to Puerto Princesa to school in June, but ten-year-old Heather joined the trio of girls who were left, and Maisie Sutherland was using a stopwatch to time how long each song took. Miss Ridderhof had said each record was only four minutes per side. In the back of the room, José and Primo kept struggling through the script. Alastair listened for a while, then thought of something. He leaned over and whispered to Miss Ridderhof, "How do we know what he's really saying in the Palawano language?"

"Good question," she whispered back. "Frankly, we don't right now. But once we get the recorder operating, we will do a reverse translation. Primo can listen to himself, then translate what he said back into Tagalog, and José can explain in English what he said. That way we know if the message is getting across." She gave a little shrug. "It would be easier if we could translate directly into the dialect we want, but . . . God usually makes a way!"

Alastair almost said, "Lastani could have translated directly from English into Palawano!" But Lastani wasn't here, and maybe it was just as well. The recorder wasn't working anyway.

Joy Ridderhof glanced hopefully over to where Ann Sherwood and Sandy Sutherland were still tinkering with the recorder, but the other woman just shook her head. "Well," Miss Ridderhof called out, "why don't we spend some time praying for this stubborn machine and rejoicing for what God is going to do next!"

Everyone—American, Scottish, Filipino—gathered around the recorder, and Miss Ridderhof began praising God for the recordings He was going to provide even yet. As their special visitor prayed, Alastair watched her from under half-closed lids. He had never met anyone who seemed so . . . so *confident*.

❖ ❖ ❖ ❖

But Sunday afternoon, after Sunday school and the morning worship service in the chapel, the recorder was still silent. Ann Sherwood switched the batteries, took out the tubes and put them back, and wiggled all the wires—but nothing seemed to work.

Joy Ridderhof refused to be discouraged. "I call this GRP—Good Rejoicing Practice," she said firmly to the little group that had gathered once again in the chapel after lunch. "The *Fortuna II* does not return until tomorrow night—that is plenty of time to still get some recordings." She glanced around at the group of disappointed faces. "My friends, even this difficulty can be an opportunity in which to demonstrate the faithfulness of God."

Alastair felt a little irritated. He wanted the recorder to work as much as anyone, but . . . what if it didn't? It seemed obvious that the thing was broken. Why did Miss Ridderhof keep everyone's hopes up?

Craigie was tugging on Miss Ridderhof's skirt. "Tell us a story!" he begged.

"Why not?" she laughed, scooping up the little boy. "Let's go outside under that palm tree, and we'll have a story."

Alastair wasn't going to stick around—he was too old for children's stories, he told himself. But even the adults seemed to relax and went out to sit under the palm tree with their American visitors. Soon

children all up and down the lanes around the chapel came running to see what was happening, until the palm tree was ringed with children of all ages like strings of sea pearls.

"I'm going to tell you a Bible story of a sister who loved her brother," Joy Ridderhof began. "The sister's name was Mary, and the brother was Lazarus—let's call him Larry."

Craigie clapped his hand on his mouth. "Larry!" he giggled.

"But Larry got very, very sick," Miss Ridderhof continued. "So sick that Mary was afraid her brother was going to die. So she sent someone to get Jesus. She knew Jesus could make her brother well again. She'd seen Him make people well! But she waited . . . and waited . . . and waited. And Jesus didn't come! And Larry died."

A chorus of childish "Ohhhs" went around the circle. Alastair tried not to feel bored. He knew this story backward and forward.

"It was very hard for Mary to understand. In fact, she didn't understand it! And when Jesus finally came, she told Him, 'If you had been here, my brother wouldn't have died!' But by then it seemed hopeless; Larry had been dead and buried for four days."

"Yeah, and he really *smelled*, too," Glen offered. The children giggled.

"But you know what, children?" Joy Ridderhof asked. "Jesus *always* had a reason for everything He did. And when we put our trust in Jesus, there is *always* hope. Do you know what Jesus did?"

Hands shot up. "He made Larry come alive again," said a dark-eyed girl. She giggled. "Mrs. Sutherland read us that story from the Bible in Sunday school."

"You're exactly right," said Miss Ridderhof. "He wanted to show the people that God was more powerful than even death."

More powerful than a broken tape recorder? Alastair wondered. He wasn't so sure God could fix *that*.

The children asked for another story, and another, but finally the group under the palm tree broke up. Once again the mountain shadows had spread like a blanket over the town. Mrs. Edwards invited the American ladies to come to their home for supper while Mr. Edwards went in search of someone more skilled who could repair the recorder.

"We'll try again this evening," Miss Ridderhof said kindly to the Sutherlands as the family prepared to return home. She laid her hand on Maisie's arm. "And don't be discouraged, dear friends. Keep on rejoicing. Rejoicing is the side of faith that laughs at impossibilities and shouts, 'It shall be done!' "

Alastair turned away and rolled his eyes. He was getting pretty sick of all this "rejoicing" business!

❖ ❖ ❖ ❖

Alastair didn't feel like talking to anyone, not even to Co-Co. He walked down to the beach and stood in the still-warm sand, watching as the waves crashed one after the other, rushed up on shore like foamy spilled milk, and then were sucked back into the sea.

The American ladies had come back from their visit to the Edwards home with an order for ten hand-crank phonographs to place in the mountain barrios. It was generous of Mr. Edwards—but what was the point? Two whole days had gone by, and the Minadyk recorder still wasn't working!

Alastair could tell his parents were worried now. There was only one day left before the *Fortuna II* returned to take Miss Ridderhof and Miss Sherwood to Puerto Princesa, then back to Manila.

Suddenly Alastair's heart began to beat a little faster. Manila. They were heading toward Manila. . . .

What if . . . ? His mind started spinning. He could travel to Manila with Miss Ridderhof and Miss Sherwood! Why not? Surely his parents couldn't object to that. His parents wouldn't get stuck in Manila if the monsoons came suddenly. Papa could do his visits to the barrios just as he'd planned. And *he* would get to boarding school after all!

Alastair let out a whoop. He'd meet lots of new kids . . . would be able to play basketball with other boys his age . . . and if he studied hard, surely he could catch up with his class.

He began running up the beach toward the house. What was it Miss Ridderhof had said this afternoon when telling the story of Lazarus? That God always had a "reason" for things that happened? Well, it sure looked like that recorder wasn't going to be recording any records! So maybe—just maybe—the "reason" they had come was to make a way for him to get to school after all!

Chapter 8

Last Chance for the Dream

CRAIGIE'S FRECKLED FACE WATCHED SOBERLY as Alastair stuffed a stack of neatly folded clothes into the canvas bag: cotton T-shirts, school shirts, shorts, socks, underwear, light jacket . . . What else did he need? Flashlight, books, Bible, pocket knife . . .

"I don'na want you to go 'way, Al'stair," said Craigie, sticking out his lower lip.

"But I gotta go to school, Craigie," Alastair said, stuffing into the canvas bag the little packet of soap, shampoo, toothbrush, and baking soda his mother had made up. "Tell you what—you feed Co-Co for me while I'm gone, okay? Sunflower seeds and water every morning. Banana, apple, and carrot for treats. But don't let Co-Co out of his cage unless Bao-Bao has been shut up in the bedroom!"

Craigie's face lit up, and he ran from the room yelling, "Glen! Glen! Al'stair says *I'm* s'posed to feed Co-Co!"

Alastair sank down on his bed and looked around the room he shared with his little brothers. He could still hardly believe his parents had agreed to let him go. His father had rubbed his chin and looked thoughtful. His mother had fussed, *"Oh, we could'na possibly presume on Miss Ridderhof!"* and *"What if he has a relapse of malaria?"* But Joy Ridderhof had beamed, *"Of course we'd be glad to escort Alastair to school! We've been staying at the Far East Broadcasting mission station in Manila—their staff children are in the school. I'll personally see to it that he gets settled."* And that was that.

Now it was Monday afternoon, and the adults had gone to the chapel one last time, praying for a miracle, hoping that even at the last minute the Minadyk recorder would come to life and they'd be able to record at least one side of a four-minute record. School had been excused for the day, but Alastair knew many of the children were hanging around the chapel, hoping to hear the "talking box."

Alastair took one last look around the room. What else should he take? His bedroll was already tied with a rattan rope. He grabbed his compass, a roll of string, and a tin box of misshapen pearls he'd collected.

He heard voices coming up the path to the cement block house—it sounded like Mr. Edwards had come back with Alastair's parents and the American visitors. Alastair ran to the front door. Did they get the Minadyk working? Had they made a recording? But one look at their faces told him the story.

It was a solemn group that sat around the Sutherland table for one last meal. Maisie Sutherland fixed a big pot of tea, and Ann Sherwood helped her slice some banana bread. Craigie crawled up in his father's lap while Glen and Heather hovered close to Joy Ridderhof.

"Are you feeling all right, Joy?" Sandy Sutherland asked, looking at her closely. "You aren't eating anything."

"Oh, nothing to worry about," she said quickly. "Just a tropical 'bug' that troubles me from time to time. You've all been so kind. I . . ." She lifted her hands in a helpless shrug. "I just hate to leave you empty-handed."

Harry Edwards let out a long sigh. "I have to admit, it's hard to understand what God is doing. I was so sure He was making a way for us to get gospel records to the Palawanos people at long last."

"You've come such a long way—for nothing!" said Maisie Sutherland. Alastair thought his mother looked about to cry.

"Oh no, not for nothing!" said Miss Ridderhof. "What wonderful friends we've made here in Brooke's Point—including these beautiful children!" She turned to Sandy Sutherland. "Your sermon on Sunday ranks with the best I've ever heard. Why, you and your wife could be pastoring a big church in Scotland, or anywhere in the English-speaking world! And yet here you serve, in a little out-of-the-way town on the southern tip of Palawan, which has no grocery stores, no hospital—"

"And it takes an airmail letter five weeks to get here from the States," groaned Ann Sherwood, rolling her eyes in mock horror. The children giggled, and everyone laughed in spite of themselves.

"No, it has not been for nothing," Joy Ridderhof said again. "Yes, we are all disappointed. But we must not let go short of victory. It would be dishonoring to God."

"Victory?" said Mr. Edwards as though he hadn't heard her correctly.

"Yes, victory! You see, it doesn't really matter if the thing promised is not given in the way we expected it. It is sure and certain because God has pledged His Word. Ann," she said to her companion, "what is that song you wrote recently?"

Ann Sherwood thought a moment, then sang in her clear, pleasant voice:

"There's a reason, a glorious reason
For everything the Lord may send your way.
When there's nothing going right,
Walk by faith, and not by sight.
There's a reason, so rejoice the livelong day."

As the last note faded away, they heard another

sound: the long, drawn-out whistle of the interisland steamer.

Reluctantly, Mr. Edwards stood up. "I better go get the carabao cart," he said. On his way out, he gave Alastair's shoulder a playful punch. "I hear you're headed off to school, young man!" He looked at the bedroll and two large canvas bags stacked by the front door. "Hmm," he teased, trying to sound light-hearted, "maybe I better make that *two* carabao carts."

Ann Sherwood went to help Maisie Sutherland make up a basket of sandwiches and fruit for the day-and-a-half journey to Puerto Princesa, their first stop. Alastair helped his father and Joy Ridderhof take the luggage outside.

"Sandy," Joy Ridderhof mused, "is Primo the only Palawanos translator you know about?"

"Why, no," said Alastair's father. "In fact, he is not the one we had hoped to use at all, but a boy, Lastani, from the same barrio. Lastani lived with us this past year and was becoming quite fluent in English. But . . . he had to leave before you arrived. He's going to the Farm School in Aborlan."

"I see," said Joy Ridderhof thoughtfully. "We missed him, then?"

"Yes, I'm afraid so. That was the first disappointment." Seeing her about to say something, Sandy Sutherland raised his hands in mock defense. "I know, I know—'guid rejoicing practice.'"

By the time the carabao cart lumbered to a stop on the main beach, twilight had turned the Sulu Sea

89

into a deep blue stage for the *Fortuna II,* riding at anchor, with a curtain of faint stars overhead. Alastair felt a little guilty feeling so excited about the boat trip ahead with everyone feeling so disappointed. But his excitement grew as his bags were transferred from the carabao cart into the boaty that was going to take him, Miss Ridderhof, and Miss Sherwood out to the steamer. *Finally!*

It was time for good-byes. Alastair got hugs from everyone, even Mr. and Mrs. Edwards. As he untangled himself from Craigie and Glen's big bear hugs, he heard his mother murmur, "Oh, Sandy. Do you think we're doing the right thing, sending Alastair off to school right now? I don't like the look of those clouds coming in from the west."

"He'll be all right, Maisie," his father said quietly. "We have to let go sometime." Alastair felt so relieved he gave his sister a big kiss on the cheek.

The boatmen carried the American ladies out to the boaty, but Alastair waded out and pulled himself over the side. "Guid-bye! Guid-bye!" he called to the little group on the shore.

Five minutes later Alastair was scrambling up the rope ladder onto the crowded deck of the *Fortuna II.* He noticed that Joy Ridderhof seemed unable to pull herself up the ladder and needed an extra hand.

"Welcome aboard, Miss Ridderhof! Miss Sherwood!" said the Filipino captain, doffing his cap. "Did you make the recordings you wanted?" he asked politely.

Ann Sherwood shook her head. "Broken recorder,"

she said, holding up the red leather case of the Minadyk.

"Is that so?" said the captain. "Terribly sorry to hear it. Say," he said, rubbing his chin thoughtfully, "there's a repairman in Brooke's Point, name of Ramos. Did he look at it?"

Alastair saw the two women look at each other and shake their heads.

"Tell you what," said the captain. "We still have some loading to do—maybe a couple of hours. Why don't you look up this man and see if he can fix your recorder?"

Again the two women looked at each other. Finally Joy Ridderhof said, "You go, Ann. I'm not feeling so well. Alastair, set our luggage over against the wheelhouse so I can sit down, will you?"

Alastair felt frustrated. They were going to just sit out here in the harbor for a couple hours while Miss Sherwood made one last-ditch effort to get the recorder fixed? Didn't these women *ever* give up?

An hour went by, and the cloud bank rolled in, dark and heavy. Soon the captain was shouting to his crew to set up tarpaulin awnings to shelter the on-deck passengers. There was no wind, but the rain began falling, and it was hard to make out the town lying along the shore.

Another hour went by. A crewman brought a cot for Miss Ridderhof, who lay down gratefully and was soon asleep. All around them, the other passengers huddled under the big tarps and ate their suppers of cold rice, smoked fish, or sandwiches. Leaning against his big canvas bag, Alastair dozed.

He awoke with a start when someone shook his shoulder. He looked up into the face of Miss Sherwood. "Miss Sherwood!" he said. "You're soaking wet! Did you—? Is it—?"

With a glance at Joy Ridderhof asleep on the cot, Ann Sherwood put a finger to her lips. "No, Alastair." She looked tired. "I've got to get out of these wet clothes. The captain is pulling up anchor. We'll be on our way now."

❖ ❖ ❖ ❖

During the night Joy Ridderhof got sicker and began to throw up. The captain graciously offered his cabin up near the wheelhouse to the two American ladies. Alastair offered to stay with the luggage on the deck. The air was warm and humid, but without any wind he was able to stay relatively dry under the huge tarp, and their canvas bags made a soft, if lumpy, bed.

The next morning—Tuesday—the rain stopped, but the clouds still hung low in the sky. The tarps were rolled back, cots folded up, and the passengers stretched their cramped muscles. "First class" passengers went belowdecks to get their breakfast from the cook's mess. Alastair rummaged in his mother's basket for a banana and a handful of nuts, then decided he should see if Miss Ridderhof and Miss Sherwood wanted some food.

Making his way up the little ladder to the smaller

upper deck that housed the wheelhouse and the crew's quarters, Alastair knocked on the door to the captain's cabin. Ann Sherwood poked her head out. "Do you want some food?" Alastair asked, holding out the basket.

Miss Sherwood shook her head. "Joy's too sick. Wait—maybe I'll have some fruit." She nodded her thanks and shut the door.

When he tired of walking the length of the small ship, Alastair settled back on his big canvas bag against the wheelhouse and watched the coast of Palawan slip past. In some places, smooth white sand ran like a sidewalk between the shore and the forest. In others, the tree-covered mountains seemed to rise right up out of the sea like a wall. From time to time they passed small barrios tucked between the forest and the shore, but mostly it was sand, trees, and mountains.

Alastair closed his eyes and thought about his family waving good-bye from the beach at Brooke's Point. But all he could see was the disappointment written all over his parents' and the Edwardses' faces—the end of Bertie's dream. He shook the image out of his mind and walked forward to the bow. The colorful sails of outrigger fishing canoes had sprouted on the sea around them.

"Why are there so many fishing boats all of a sudden?" he asked a crewman nearby.

"We'll be passing Aborlan soon," said the crewman. "Home base for these fishermen."

Aborlan? That's where Lastani was going to

school! Alastair felt a rush of blood to his head. The *Fortuna II* didn't stop until Puerto Princesa that evening. But . . . why couldn't it? How long would it take to send a boaty to shore with three passengers? They could find Lastani, make the recordings, and . . . and catch up to the *Fortuna II* in Puerto Princesa. He'd heard Miss Ridderhof say they were going to lay over in Palawan's "capital city" for a few days before they headed on to Manila anyway. Alastair could just see Mr. Edwards' face when he heard that Bertie's dream wasn't dead after all!

There was no time to lose. Alastair flew up the little ladder to the upper deck and banged on the door to the captain's cabin. The door flew open, and Miss Sherwood's usually mild eyes flashed. "Alastair! What—"

"I've got to talk to Miss Ridderhof right away!" he said.

"No, no. She's too sick to talk. Please, Alastair—come back later." And the door shut in his face.

Alastair stepped backward. Didn't they realize they were passing their chance to get the Palawano recordings? Then a new idea put his feet into action.

He ran along the narrow gangway and slipped into the wheelhouse. The Filipino captain was looking through a pair of binoculars at the horizon, while his first mate gripped the big wheel that guided the interisland steamer.

"Captain?" said Alastair, his voice urgent, shrill. "Can you make a stop at Aborlan? The two ladies—the Americans—there's a boy in Aborlan who can help them! It's verra important! If you don'na stop, their trip is all for nothing!"

The captain continued to stare out the windows of the wheelhouse with the binoculars. Alastair realized he wasn't looking toward the coast of Palawan, but sweeping the horizon, out to sea.

"Captain!" he tried again.

"Stop at Aborlan?" the captain broke in without turning around. "Impossible. There's a monsoon brewing out there. We've got to get to safe harbor in Puerto Princesa as quickly as possible."

Alastair's shoulders sagged. He stepped outside the wheelhouse in time to see large clusters of bamboo houses intermingled with cement block buildings slipping past along the shore. Aborlan. He watched glumly until the town disappeared from sight.

Then he sighed. What did it matter anyway? The Minadyk recorder was still dead. Without it, Bertie's dream was dead, too.

Chapter 9

The Kidnapping Plot

THE *FORTUNA II* STEAMED into Puerto Princesa Bay that evening, ahead of the storm that still hung low on the horizon. Sitting on their pile of luggage in front of the wheelhouse, Alastair watched Palawan Island's capital city take shape along the north shore of the bay, a pretty jumble of fishing docks, office buildings, small shops, Spanish-style homes, and traditional Filipino bamboo huts on stilts. The bay, which was about two miles across, was a beehive of activ-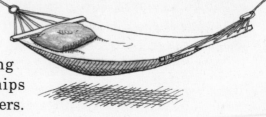ity—fishing vintas and small boatys dodging larger cargo ships and tramp steamers.

"Any of your mother's goodies left in that basket?" said a woman's familiar voice. "Or did you eat them all?"

Alastair turned to see a pale but smiling Joy Ridderhof steadying herself on the ship's rail behind him. "Miss Ridderhof!" he said. "You're feeling better?"

She nodded and sank down onto the luggage. "A little shaky. But I'm rejoicing! Sometimes these tropical 'bugs' put me in bed for days at a time."

"I guess we'll be getting off soon," Alastair hinted, passing his mother's basket to Miss Ridderhoff. No one had said anything about where they were going to stay or what they were going to do in Puerto Princesa.

"Yes," she said, peeking in the basket. "I hope Mr. Alvior will be here to meet us—we stayed in his home on our way to Brooke's Point. Oh." Joy Ridderhof laid the basket aside without taking anything. "Ann told me you wanted to talk to me earlier today."

Alastair hesitated, then shrugged. "It . . . was nothing." What good would it do to tell her his idea now?

The *Fortuna II*'s engines reversed, then came to stop as the steamer eased alongside one of the docks jutting into the bay. Soon a gangplank had been laid from the deck to the dock, and passengers began getting off, lugging their bags and boxes with them. Alastair noticed that several Filipino policemen were checking people's travel papers as they got off.

Ann Sherwood arrived just then with an armload of their belongings from the captain's cabin. "I don't want you carrying anything," she scolded Joy. "You just get off and find Mr. Alvior; Alastair and I will take care of the bags. And hold on to that railing!" she hollered after her friend as Joy obediently headed for the gangplank.

❖ ❖ ❖ ❖

Alastair sighed contentedly, swinging in a hammock on the front patio of the Alviors' neat wooden house, surrounded by hanging plants and sweet-smelling, flowering bushes. He had never eaten such a wonderful meal! But he noticed that Joy Ridderhof had barely touched her *adobo*, a rich stew of chicken and pork. She fared better on Mrs. Alvior's *leche flan*—an egg custard—for dessert.

The Alviors were Filipino Christians who pastored a little church in Puerto Princesa. He was a serious-looking man, with glasses and a slight stoop; his wife was eager and talkative. They peppered their American friends with questions about their adventures in Brooke's Point—and exclaimed in disappointment and disbelief when they heard the women had to leave empty-handed.

But Ann Sherwood, acting like a dorm mother and drill sergeant combined, had ordered Joy off to bed right after supper, and now Alastair could hear her quietly talking with the Alviors inside.

"Joy always says, 'God has His reasons,' " she was saying, "but it's hard to understand in this case."

Does'na anyone see? Alastair thought. *God is making a way for me to get to school!*

"Mostly I feel badly for Mr. Edwards," Ann Sherwood continued, her voice tinged with sadness. "He had carried his son's dream in his heart for so long."

"Yes, yes, a shame," said Mrs. Alvior. "The Palawanos tribes desperately need the Gospel in their own language."

Alastair was glad he hadn't said anything. His "reason" would sound pretty selfish.

"The boy in Aborlan . . ." It was Mr. Alvior's voice. "That's only thirty miles away as the crow flies. Maybe we could hire a jeepney—"

"I thought of that," said Miss Sherwood. "But Joy isn't up to traveling tomorrow. She should rest, get her strength back. Then we must take the steamer on to Manila. When did you say it was leaving?"

"Maybe Thursday, maybe Friday—who knows?" Mrs. Alvior's sweet voice held a note of concern. "There are rumors that the Huk rebels from Luzon are hiding out on some of the other islands. The police have started searching all incoming and outgoing ships."

So that's what those policemen were doing, thought Alastair.

He heard Miss Sherwood sigh. "It hardly makes any difference. The Minadyk isn't working."

"Don't you worry about that machine!" said Mr. Alvior. "I know a repairman who is very, very good with sound equipment. I will take it to him myself tomorrow."

"I hope so," said Ann Sherwood. "We still have a few more languages we want to record before we leave the

Philippines. It is so strange . . . so strange. We got it repaired just before we went to Brooke's Point. But once we got there, it never even flickered. See?"

Alastair heard a chair scrape and the sound of footsteps. Miss Sherwood was probably going to show them the defective recorder. He gave a push with his foot dangling off the side of the hammock and swung lazily back and forth, watching the lanterns on half a dozen fishing boats heading out of the bay for the night's fishing. He wondered why there weren't more of them. . . . Maybe the storm warnings had scared them off.

"Wha—?" Miss Sherwood's voice broke into his thoughts. "It . . . it's working! See that green light?"

Alastair nearly fell out of the hammock. The recorder was *working*?

"Oh no . . . it went off again."

Alastair sank back into the hammock once more. But his mind was still on fast forward. If the recorder really could be fixed . . . if they could go back down the coast to Aborlan tomorrow . . . no, no, that wouldn't work. Miss Ridderhof was too weak to travel tomorrow.

Alastair stared at the fishing boats still heading out of the harbor. Some of the small lights headed south once they cleared the mouth of the bay.

Suddenly he sat up straight and swung both feet off the hammock. If Miss Ridderhof couldn't go to Lastani, why couldn't Lastani come to her?

✧ ✧ ✧ ✧

Alastair jumped to the ground from the window-sill, tiptoed through the bushes surrounding the Alviors' house, then set out for the waterfront at a trot. Sneaking out had been almost too easy. He had said good-night to Miss Sherwood and the Alviors, closed the door to the little storeroom where they'd set up a cot for him, and slid quietly out the window. No one would miss him until morning.

His plan made him feel excited, reckless. If he could find a fishing boat that would take him down the coast to Aborlan, find Lastani, and hitch a ride back to Puerto Princesa with the returning fishermen, he might be back by breakfast! Wouldn't Miss Ridderhof be surprised when he showed up with Lastani?

Somewhere at the back of his mind, a little voice nagged him: *This plan is crazy, and you know it!* Alastair pushed it away. Instead, he tried to keep track of the turns he made—left, right, right again, left—so he could remember how to get back to the Alviors' house.

Soon he was running along the waterfront, looking for a fishing boat that looked like it might still be going out to sea. "Hey, mister!" he called to a bare-footed man who was rolling up a huge net in the bow of his large outrigger canoe. "Are you heading south toward Aborlan?"

"Not tonight," the man called back. "See that storm coming?" He turned back to his net.

Alastair asked another fisherman, and another. All shook their heads. "I'll pay!" he said, fingering the money in his pocket that his father had given him to help buy food on the way to Manila. This brought shrugs, but still no takers.

"Ask that trawler over by the dock," an old man said, jerking his head toward a weather-beaten motorboat with a small cabin on the deck. "Heard they were going south."

Alastair ran down the long dock to where three Filipino men in dirty T-shirts and loose pants were getting ready to cast off. "I want to go to Aborlan! Will you take me?" he yelled over low chugging of the vessel's diesel engine.

One of the men with a straggly gray moustache looked at him hard. "You got family in Aborlan, schoolboy?"

"Nay," Alastair admitted. "I'm . . . I'm from Brooke's Point, but I'm supposed to meet a friend in Aborlan. It's verra important! I need to go tonight."

"Listen to that Scots accent," snickered another man, younger, his head wrapped in a yellow cloth. Then he said something in a dialect Alastair didn't understand.

The three men looked at each other and spoke quickly in the strange dialect. Alastair jiggled the coins in his pocket impatiently. Were they going to take him or not? Then the older man motioned to Alastair. "Get on board, be queek about it. You're lucky we have to go to Aborlan tonight. But don't get in the way."

Alastair scrambled over the side and settled himself on a coil of rope. He could hardly believe his good luck. His plan was working!

The twenty-four-foot trawler backed away from the dock, eased its bow toward the mouth of the bay, and headed into the inky night. Alastair looked back at the shore, its twinkling lights growing smaller and smaller. When they turned around the lip of the bay, the lights snuffed out altogether.

Suddenly Alastair felt a flicker of fear. He was alone on a boat with three total strangers, and no one back at the Alviors—or his family, for that matter—knew where he was or whom he was with. How stupid! How utterly stupid he was!

But the men seemed to ignore him. The older man stayed at the wheel, peering into the darkness. He was staying fairly close to shore; Alastair could hear waves breaking against the rugged shoreline.

The wind had picked up, and Alastair hunkered down on the coil of rope, trying to get below the spray of the sea. The trawler rose and plunged on the swells. The boy tried to think what he was going to do when he got to Aborlan. It would be the middle of the night—how would he find the Farm School? He might have to wait till morning. And Lastani ... what would Lastani think of his plan when he did find him? He'd been assuming all along that Lastani would be glad to return with him to Puerto Princesa to do the translating. But ... what if he didn't believe that the American woman had come? Ravi, the Moros boy, had told him it was all a big lie and that Alastair's family and Mr. Edwards just wanted to exploit the Palawanos people. Maybe Lastani wouldn't want to translate the Christian message for his people now.

Alastair closed his eyes, trying to shut out his doubts and fears. He felt very tired, very, very tired. . . .

✧ ✧ ✧ ✧

A spray of cold water in his face woke Alastair with a start. Someone had covered him with a waterproof slicker, but his clothes were damp, and he was shivering. The wind had picked up, driving heaving waves before it like a cowboy with an unruly herd of cattle.

Alastair tried to get his bearings. He couldn't see the shore in the pitch-dark night—only flashes of foam as the waves broke against the invisible shoreline. No one else was on deck. But there was a light in the cabin, and he could hear voices inside.

Pushing aside the slicker, Alastair crept closer to the open cabin door, holding on to the gunwale as the boat pitched side to side with each wave. Now he could see the older man peering through the front windows of the cabin as he steered with the inside wheel. The younger man with the yellow turban was gesturing and talking, probably to the third man, whom Alastair couldn't see. Alastair crouched close to the cabin door and strained to hear what they were saying.

"What do you think they'll pay for the runt?" Yellow Head was saying.

"Whatever we ask, you fool," said the invisible voice. "They'll want the kid back. And that other guy down there—the American—he's a rich capitalist. He'll raise the money somehow."

Yellow Head let out a whoop. "And to think the kid walked right up to us and begged us to take him! Those American dollars are going to swell the Huk treasury."

"Shut up!" snapped the man at the wheel. "We gotta think this thing through. This storm is going to break any minute—we're going to need shelter some-where."

Alastair flattened himself against the outside wall of the cabin, his breath coming in short gasps. He was being kidnapped by Huk rebels!

"Isn't that blinking light ahead Aborlan?" said the invisible voice. "Maybe we ought to pull in there after all."

"Can't," said the pilot's voice. "The word might be out by now that the boy is missing. Someone's ex-pecting him in Aborlan—isn't that what he said? Too risky. We'll find a barrio down the coast a ways, hide out for a few days."

Alastair twisted his head and looked around the edge of the cabin. Sure enough, a light was blinking beyond the line of foaming breakers off the boat's starboard. But they weren't going to stop! He had to get off this boat—now.

His heart beating wildly, Alastair looked franti-cally about the deck. Hooked to the side was a life ring. Easing himself away from the cabin, Alastair made his way along the gunwale and unhooked the ring with shaking fingers. The wind was blowing

from the east straight toward Palawan Island—
surely the wind and waves would carry him to shore.

He slid his head and shoulders through the ring,
sat on the gunwale, and taking a deep breath, threw
himself into the sea. Immediately a wave crashed
over his head, and he came up coughing. As he shook
water out of his eyes, he looked back toward the
trawler. He saw figures running out of the cabin and
thought he heard a shout.

Then another wave crashed over him, and the
boat was gone.

Chapter 10

Race to the Bay

ALASTAIR HAD NO IDEA how long he lay on the sand. He blinked open his eyes, but the world was still dark. Rain pelted his skin like stinging nettles. He didn't want to move, but the tide . . . he had to get away from the tide. Struggling out of the life ring, he painfully pulled himself on hands and knees farther away from the crashing waves behind him. In the darkness, he felt sharp blades of grass beneath his hands, then bumped up against the scaly bark of a coconut palm. With a groan of relief, he collapsed at the foot of the tree and lost consciousness.

A strong hand was shaking his shoulder. Alastair opened his eyes and stared into the lined, weather-beaten face of an old man. As Alastair struggled to sit up, the man grinned widely, revealing several missing teeth; the rest were stained with betel-nut juice.

A steel-gray daylight lit the beach. The rain had stopped, but the clouds still hung low and the wind whipped the palm fronds above Alastair's head like a crowd of children at fiesta, frantically waving their hands to grab candy being tossed in the air. The man kept saying something Alastair didn't understand and lifted him to his feet.

For the first time, Alastair noticed his shoes were gone, and he had only one sock. Sand clung to his wet shirt and shorts. He pulled off the sock and, with the man's arm around him, let the old man lead him slowly down a grassy path.

In a few minutes they came to a cluster of thatched bamboo huts in a little clearing, standing off the ground on stilts. Pigs, chickens, and even a few goats wandered underneath the huts. A large fishing net needing repair was strung between two palm trees. Off to the side, several canoes without their outrigger pontoons lay on their sides.

A swarm of dark-haired children stared as the old man half pushed Alastair up the ladder to the porch of his hut. He went inside and came back a moment later with a handwoven blanket, which he put around the boy's shoulders. He disappeared once more and brought back a wooden bowl of thin white liquid. Gratefully, Alastair tipped the bowl to his mouth. Coconut milk.

The milk seemed to send strength through

Alastair's blood, and his mind cleared. He had escaped from the Huk rebels. He hadn't drowned. He was safe on land. But . . . *where* was he? He coughed a couple times, then tried to speak. "Aborlan?" he asked the old man. "Is this Aborlan?"

The man just looked at him for a moment, puzzled. Then he flashed his brown-stained teeth. "*Si! Si!* Aborlan!" And he pointed through the trees.

Relief flooded through Alastair's exhausted body. He knew Aborlan was a bigger town than this little cluster of fishing huts. The town must be nearby. He tried again through chattering teeth. "I have a f-f-friend . . . at the Farm School." The man looked puzzled, then shrugged. Alastair's head sank into his hands. How was he going to make the man understand?

The man stood up, rattled off a string of words at one of the children gawking up at the strange boy with freckled skin and copper hair. The child ran off. A short while later, the child returned with a young woman in her twenties wearing a flowing skirt, an embroidered white blouse, and a colorful scarf covering her long, dark hair.

"Hello!" she said in English, her eyes wide open in genuine surprise. "So you are the 'fish' Grandfather dragged from the sea this morning."

"Oh! I'm verra g-g-glad you speak English," said Alastair, scrambling to his feet. Many Filipinos in the towns spoke both English and Filipino, the official languages in the Philippines, even though there were dozens of different dialects scattered over the islands. "I . . . I fell off a boat. But I must g-get to the

Farm School in Aborlan. Do you know where it is?"

The young woman raised one eyebrow. "You just 'fell' off a boat? Hmm, I see." She seemed skeptical. But to Alastair's relief she asked no more questions. "Yes, I can take you to the Farm School. But we must hurry, because I need to go to work." She turned to the old man. "Thank you, Grandfather! I will take the boy now. Come, come—we must hurry."

Alastair bowed his thanks to the old man, then scrambled down the ladder and hurried after the young woman, who was disappearing between the trees.

❖ ❖ ❖ ❖

Alastair didn't know whether to laugh or cry when he saw the tall young man striding toward him. Lastani's long hair had been cut short; otherwise he looked the same. Suddenly all the doubts and fears of the past twelve hours were washed away in a flood of relief. He had found Lastani! Everything was going to be all right now.

"Alastair!" said the Palawanos boy in astonishment. "Why you here? How you come?"

Alastair looked nervously at the principal of the Farm School, who stood on the covered porch of the school office, watching them. "All right," the man said, waving them away. "You boys talk. Then come see me, Lastani, all right?" He disappeared into the office.

The boys walked over to a wooden bench. "Joy Ridderhof—she came!" Alastair said, the words coming out in a rush. "But the recorder did'na work. And now she's in Puerto Princesa. And I've come for you! You must come with me—today!"

Lastani stared at him. "Alastair, you talking crazy talk. Look at you—your clothes wet. You shivering. You no shoes. Did you walk? Did you swim? There was storm last night! Where is father and mother?"

Alastair blinked to keep back tears. He was tired. He was hungry. He didn't feel very good. But taking a big breath, Alastair started at the beginning. . . .

". . . And an old fisherman found me on the beach, and here I am," Alastair finished after telling the whole story. "Please, Lastani, you *must* come back with me to Puerto Princesa right away, before Miss Ridderhof leaves for Manila. It's our last chance to make gospel records for your people!"

Lastani stood up and paced back and forth, his fingers gripping the lambos good-luck charm around his neck. "Why these records so important? I can't leave Farm School just because you come foolish. But," he whirled on Alastair, "American ladies sick with worry by now. You—you such fool. You could be killed now—or drowned!" He rolled his eyes, then resumed pacing, muttering to himself.

Then he stopped. "I must take you back to American lady. What I must do." With that, Lastani ran up the path to the school office and disappeared inside.

❖ ❖ ❖

It had never occurred to Alastair *how* they were going to get back to Puerto Princesa. The idea of returning with a fishing boat now seemed impossible. But as they turned out of the gate of the school and headed north along the coastal road, Alastair looked up at Lastani in surprise. "We're going to walk?"

Lastani snorted. "Do you have carabao cart? Or horse? Maybe motor car hidden in bushes."

"But . . ." Alastair looked at his bare feet plodding along the muddy, rutted road. He would never be able to walk thirty miles with no shoes. Even *with* shoes, how long would it take? Ten hours? Fifteen?

Alastair pressed his lips together tightly. He already looked like a foolish little boy in Lastani's eyes. He wasn't going to complain now.

The two boys walked steadily along the dirt road that ran along the coast. Sometimes they could see the sea, gray and choppy under a dull sky. At other times the road ran into the forest, passing small barrios full of chattering children and carabao carts loaded with coconuts, bananas, or palm fronds to repair the thatched roof houses. Alastair was grateful when Lastani called a halt and opened up the packet of food the school cook had tied up in a cloth sling. He gave Alastair some cold rice cakes, and they shared a smoked fish. Out of habit, Alastair bowed his head to say a quick blessing on the food. When he looked up, Lastani was staring at him.

All too soon, they were back on their feet. But the food revived Alastair's spirits, and he swung along the rutted road, trying to ignore the blister forming on his foot. "Wind rising," said Lastani, looking at the swaying treetops. Sure enough, the sky opened and sheets of rain drove in from the sea, soaking both boys. Lastani grabbed Alastair's shirt and pulled him along so they wouldn't get separated in the storm.

Gradually the rain eased, but walking was more difficult now in the wet, muddy road. How long had they been traveling? Alastair put one foot in front of the other, trying to ignore the aches in his legs. Left, right, left, right ... "guid rejoicing practice" ... slog through the mud ... dodge that puddle ... "guid rejoicing practice" ...

Suddenly, out of nowhere it seemed, a jeepney came roaring toward them, blowing its jarring horn. The boys barely had time to jump out of the way before the jeep-like bus, painted a garish red and yellow, with swirls and mirrors and reflectors decorating its hood and windshield, bounced past them, sending a spray of mud all over them. A handful of passengers waved and hollered out the open windows as they passed ... and then the boys stood staring at its tailgate, bouncing over the ruts as it disappeared around a bend.

"Do you think it'll come back?" Alastair said hopefully. Lastani shrugged.

After another rest and eating the last of the rice cakes, the boys plodded on. Alastair lost all track of time. How many hours had gone by since the jeepney had passed? One? Two? He concentrated on a tree at the side of the road up ahead till they passed it, then picked another point to reach for, as if pulling himself along by an invisible rope.

And then they heard it again, the roar of a jeepney

engine behind them. Soon the garish vehicle bounced
into sight again, blaring its horn for them to get out

of the way. But instead, Lastani faced the jeepney in the middle of the road and waved it to a stop. The driver braked to a noisy stop and peered at them through the open door.

"Can we ride?" Lastani asked, his voice hoarse and weary.

"Can you pay?" said the driver.

Alastair shoved his hand into the pocket of his shorts. Most of the pocket money he was going to use to pay the fishing boat for passage had disappeared. But he came up with several coins and held them out. He could hardly stop his hand from shaking.

The driver started to shake his head. Then suddenly he jerked his thumb. "Come on. Get in."

The boys sank into the hard wooden seats of the jeepney as if they were plush cushions. Alastair leaned his head against the metal window frame. His head hurt. He had never felt so tired. He wished he could lie down and go to sleep for a long time. . . .

"Alastair, wake up!" said Lastani's voice. "We have to get off."

Alastair tried to open his eyes, but he felt so dizzy. He felt Lastani pull him to his feet and half drag him off the jeepney until they were standing on the road once more. The driver was bent down looking underneath the bus. "Broken axle," the man muttered.

"How far Puerto Princesa?" Lastani said to the driver.

"Not far—a mile or two to this side of the bay."

"Many thanks." Lastani's voice took on a gentle

tone. "Alastair, come. I help you."

With Lastani's strong arm around him, Alastair managed to put one foot in front of the other. Only a mile or two . . . they were going to make it now.

Afternoon shadows started to lengthen across the road. Shadows? Alastair looked up. The clouds had broken, and sunshine bathed the dripping trees. Yes, yes, they were going to make it now.

"There is big bay," said Lastani. The boys stopped. They were standing on a small bluff, looking down at the bay, which stretched maybe two miles across. The colorful sails of dozens of fishing canoes dotted the water. On the other side lay Puerto Princesa. The road they'd been walking on curved away to their left, making its long way around the bay.

"We save time—we find fisherman, take us across," said Lastani. He tightened his grip around Alastair and started down toward the shoreline. The hoot of a ship's whistle floated across the water. Suddenly Lastani stopped. "Look!" he said and pointed.

Alastair stared. An interisland steamer was blasting its horn and heading toward the mouth of the bay. He couldn't read its name, but he knew what it was: the *Fortuna II*. The ship taking Miss Ridderhof and Miss Sherwood on to Manila. The ship he was supposed to be on.

The last ounce of energy drained from Alastair's feverish body.

They were too late.

Chapter 11

The Gospel Atom Bomb

DUSK WAS SWALLOWING UP THE ISLAND as Lastani and Alastair crawled out of the outrigger fishing canoe that had brought them across the bay. Lights were springing up in the homes and other buildings of Puerto Princesa. "Where is home of Mr. Alvior?" Lastani demanded. "I know you are sick, but use head, Alastair—*use head!*"

Alastair stared dully at the street that had brought him down to the docks just twenty-four hours earlier. What was the point? Miss Ridderhof and Miss Sherwood were gone, on their way back to Manila. He had tried to tell Lastani he was sorry he had made him walk so far for noth-

ing, to go back to Aborlan—but Lastani had refused to listen as he said, "Mr. Alvior only person you know Puerto Princesa? You say he is good man? I take you there. He will get you home again."

Alastair's head hurt. Could he remember what turns he had made? "I . . . I think I turned left, right, right again, then left," he said uncertainly.

"Coming from Mr. Alvior's house?" said Lastani. "Then we go back opposite way—turn right, then left, left again, then right," he said. And with Alastair leaning against him, the older boy started up the first street.

The streets seemed so much longer to Alastair than they had just one night before when he had trotted the whole way down to the bay. But finally Lastani said, "Last turn. What house, Alastair?"

Alastair just wanted to lie down. He didn't care where. The road would be fine. But he tried to concentrate, peering closely at the tidy little homes they were passing—not bamboo huts like in the barrios, but wood or cement block, tucked in among the palms and fruit trees, softened by leafy ferns, spreading ivy, and different varieties of orchids.

"There." He pointed listlessly. "The hammock on the patio—"

Alastair sagged against the doorframe as Lastani knocked. He dreaded the scolding he was sure to get, but he could endure it if only they would let him lie down.

The door opened. Petite Mrs. Alvior looked at Lastani and said, "Yes? May I help you?" Then she saw his companion. Her eyes widened. "Alastair?" In an instant she had disappeared, leaving the two boys standing outside, and they could hear her voice calling, "Miss Ridderhof! He's back! He's back!"

Alastair felt confused. Was it the fever? He thought she said Miss Ridderhof—

Then Joy Ridderhof was standing at the door, her silvery hair shining in the lamplight behind her. "Oh, Alastair," she said. "You have given us such a fright."

"I . . . I went to get Lastani," mumbled Alastair, summoning his last bit of strength.

"I know," she said softly.

❖ ❖ ❖ ❖

Every time Alastair awoke during the night, too hot one minute, shivering the next, he wondered why Miss Ridderhof was still in Puerto Princesa. And what did she mean by "I know"? But the American missionary had insisted that he go right to bed after giving him some of the malaria medicine his parents had packed in his bags, and there had been no time to ask or answer questions.

When he woke up in the morning, wind and rain were lashing at the little window in the storeroom—typical for August in the Philippines. He could hear voices in the sitting room. It sounded like Lastani and Miss Ridderhof, but he couldn't make out the words. He struggled to get up, but all his muscles felt like dead weights. He fell back on the pillow and slept again.

The next time Alastair opened his eyes, Joy Ridderhof was sitting on the end of the cot in the storeroom, smiling. "It's time for your medicine, young man," she said, handing him a white tablet and a glass of water.

"The *Fortuna II* . . . we saw it leaving," said Alastair. "I thought you were gone."

She pulled her rimless eyeglasses down on her nose and looked at him over the tops. "You didn't *really* think we'd just leave you behind, did you?"

He wrinkled his forehead. "I . . . I guess I did'na think. I just thought we'd missed you, that we got here too late." He took another swallow of water. "But . . . how did you know I went to get Lastani?"

Miss Ridderhof smiled again. "We guessed. When we woke up yesterday morning and discovered that you had just . . . disappeared, we went down to the waterfront and asked the captain of the *Fortuna II* if he'd seen you since we arrived in Puerto Princesa. He said no, but he *did* say that you had tried to get him to stop at Aborlan, and you seemed very upset when he didn't. In the meantime, Mr. Alvior was asking people if they'd seen a boy with copper-colored hair. Several fishermen said you had asked them to take you south last night, before the storm broke. So we just put two and two together. But"— her face got very serious—"we were very worried, Alastair, and from the tale Lastani tells, we had good reason to be."

Alastair hung his head. "I . . . I'm sorry I made you worry, and—"

"Shh, that's enough," she said. "We can talk more when that fever's gone."

As the door shut behind her, Alastair pulled the sheet up around his chin. He felt very depressed. He not only made her worry, but he'd made his American friends miss the steamer to Manila. He had ruined his chance to get to school and had gotten sick again with malaria. For what? The recorder was probably still broken, which meant . . .

Bringing Lastani was all for nothing.

❖ ❖ ❖ ❖

Light was fading in the little storeroom when Alastair sat up, trying to shake sleep from his eyes. Had the whole day gone by already? Then he realized his head didn't hurt, and the fever seemed to be gone.

Wrapping the sheet around him like a blanket, Alastair opened the door to the little storeroom and peeked into the kitchen. Empty. But he heard Lastani's voice in the sitting room, but it sounded strange. Slowly Alastair made his way to the open door.

Inside the sitting room, Mr. and Mrs. Alvior were sitting together on a wicker sofa, nodding their heads and looking at each other as if something wonderful was happening. Lastani and Joy Ridderhof were sitting at one end of a table; Ann Sherwood sat at the other end, the red leather case of the Minadyk open in front of her. Alastair could hear Lastani speaking

in Palawano—but when Alastair looked at him, Lastani was listening, not talking.

Lastani's voice was coming from the red leather case.

"The recorder!" Alastair gasped out loud. "It's working!"

Five pairs of eyes looked toward the doorway.

Ann Sherwood snapped off the recorder and smiled. "Off and on, but—yes! It's working. In fact, when we took it to the repair shop yesterday and turned it on, the little green light shone steadily like we'd never had a day of trouble! But the repairman did find a broken wire, which he fixed."

"But—"

"Come sit down, Alastair," said Joy Ridderhof. "We are checking our translation." She turned to Lastani. "Let's go back to the beginning, Lastani. Listen to the words you have recorded in Palawano, then tell us in English what you have said."

Alastair curled up in a fat, overstuffed chair and listened as Ann Sherwood turned the recorder back on and flipped the playback switch. Lastani's voice, speaking his own Palawano language easily and confidently, filled the room. After several moments, Ann Sherwood stopped the recorder. "Lastani?"

Lastani had a look of awe on his face as he translated his words in Palawano back into English. "Chief of Sky, God, He who made sky and earth and all in it, He has sent already a message to all people of the world. This message is in bundle of leaves they call 'Bundle of Leaves What Chief of Sky Says.' It tells how Chief of Sky gave His Son; He has only one Son, come to earth to receive punishment of our sins. He love us very much, so much He died on a tree tied crosswise so that we not receive punishment in wicked barrio down below, place of fire and torment forever. . . ."

Alastair listened. Hearing Lastani's simple words,

it was almost as if he were hearing the gospel message for the first time.

Back and forth went Lastani's Palawano words on the recorder, and his English translation. "Men and women needed someone who could take away evil and sin from their hearts. Finally, God came down to this world to do this himself. He became a man. In this form He was called the Son of God. He was holy. He did no sin. He healed the sick. He fed the people when they were hungry. He did great miracles that only God could do. . . ."

To Alastair's surprise, tears were running down Mr. Alvior's cheeks as he listened.

"But wicked people nailed Son of God to tree tied crosswise. He gave himself into their hands so that He could suffer for us. They killed Him and buried Him. But since He was God as well as man, He rose up after three days, and in a little while He went back to God's Home in Heaven. . . ."

A smile started deep within Alastair and spread over his face. He finally understood Bertie Edwards' dream. He could imagine the gum gatherers in the mountains, sitting around a hand-crank record player, listening to these words—God's words—for the first time in their lives. It almost made it worth— no, it *was* worth not going to school in Manila until next year.

"Now by believing in Yesu Krist, God's Son, we are saved from our sins. Receive Him as your Savior, and you will go to God's Home in Heaven after you die, to live forever with God. What God says, He will do."

Ann Sherwood clicked off the tape recorder. "Now if we can contact the girls from Brooke's Point who are going to school here in Puerto Princesa, and if they remember the songs in Palawano they practiced, we can add gospel music to this tape!"

Mr. Alvior jumped up. "Yes, yes! We will bring the girls here." He was so excited he could hardly stand still. "We have prayed and prayed for many years that God would send us help to reach the tribal people who have not heard God's Word. Now God has sent you women to bring us this new weapon of spiritual warfare—records in the languages of the people. It is the atom bomb of the Gospel!"

"Yes, God is faithful," said Joy Ridderhof, deeply moved. She turned to Lastani. "I guess God really did have His 'reasons' for why the recorder didn't work at Brooke's Point. He had prepared *you* to be our translator!"

Everyone laughed. Alastair hugged his knees. Wouldn't his parents and Mr. Edwards jump for joy when they heard that the Palawano recordings had been made after all?

"Lastani," Joy Ridderhof went on, "when I wrote Mr. Edwards, I promised to pay a translator for all the hard work. I would like to pay you now."

Alastair grinned. He'd almost forgotten about the pay. Now Lastani could get the 'good knife' he'd wanted so badly.

But to Alastair's surprise, Lastani shook his head. "No, no," he said softly. "If Son of God, Jesus, give so much to me and my people—His own life—

then I translate these words for you, no charge. It was for Jesus."

✧ ✧ ✧ ✧

On Joy Ridderhof's orders, Alastair had gone back to bed. But there was still something he had to do. When she came to the storeroom with his final dose of medicine, he said, "Miss Ridderhof, I'm . . . I'm really sorry I made you miss the steamer to Manila."

"But we didn't," she said casually. "The *Fortuna II* has several other stops to make on some of the smaller islands and is due back here in a few days. Hopefully you'll be well enough to travel by then. In the meantime, Mr. Alvior is going to help us record several more dialects in this area." She smiled. "We should have you in school by next week. Good night, Alastair."

Chapter 12

The Talking Box
(Manila, Luzon Island, 1951)

THERE'S A DELIVERY FOR YOU, Sutherland," said one of the older boys, stopping by Alastair's table in the school dining hall. "And I mean a *big* one."

Alastair put down his fork. A delivery? He'd already gotten a box from his mother for his thirteenth birthday a couple months before. Who else would send him anything? He shrugged at his classmates, who were looking at him enviously, and pushed back his chair.

It was almost time for the school term to end. In seven months Alastair had almost caught up with his classmates for the three months he had missed. He looked

around at the whitewashed school buildings as he walked over to the office. It had been hard work, but it was worth it. And basketball was the greatest! In two years he could try out for the basketball team.

Alastair pushed open the door to the school office. Sure enough, two large wooden packing crates were stacked in a corner. "Somebody said I had a—"

"Delivery, yes," said the school secretary, peering over the top of her glasses, which had rhinestones decorating the upswept corners and were fastened to a cord that hung around her neck. "Arrived by freighter from the States just today. Here—" She handed him two sheets of paper stapled together. "This shipping notice came with them."

Alastair went over to the crates and looked at the labels. One said, "To Mr. Harry Edwards, Brooke's Point, Palawan Island, Philippines." The other said, "To Pastor Alvior, Puerto Princesa, Palawan Island." The crates were stamped GOSPEL RECORDINGS, U.S.A. in big red letters.

He glanced at the sheets of paper, marked "Bill of Lading." The one to Harry Edwards listed "Ten hand-crank phonographs . . . Ten sets of records, Palawano dialect." The contents of the crate headed for Puerto Princesa were similar, except the records had been done in different dialects.

"Finally," Alastair murmured. "Bertie's dream come true."

The school secretary was still peering at him

curiously over the top of her pointy glasses. "Records," he said with a shrug and a little smile.

"Records?" she echoed. She adjusted her glasses to look at the two large boxes. "You must have a mighty big collection, is all I can say."

❖ ❖ ❖ ❖

Alastair leaned over the railing of the interisland steamer, searching the crowd that was waiting for the small ship to dock. Would he see a familiar face? He'd written the Farm School, telling Lastani when he was due to come home. But was Lastani coming home, too?

Suddenly he saw them—a tall boy and a short man. "Lastani!" he yelled, waving his arms back and forth. "Mr. Alvior! Up here!"

The glittering blue water of Puerto Princesa Bay lay bathed in April sunshine. Alastair was on his way home for the two-month-long school holiday. The *Luzon Queen* was going to stop in Puerto Princesa for only six hours before it headed south down the coast of Palawan. But that was all right with Alastair—he was eager to get home to Brooke's Point.

He had to wait until all the Puerto Princesa passengers got off. But finally Lastani came banging up the metal gangplank, carrying two canvas bags, with Mr. Alvior right behind him.

"Alastair!" grinned the Palawanos boy. "This time you travel something little bigger, little safer than fishing boat of Huk rebels, I see!"

Alastair's face turned red. Lastani *would* have to tease him about that.

Mr. Alvior shook his hand, beaming from ear to ear. "I understand you have something for me from Miss Ridderhof," the Filipino pastor said, hardly able to contain his excitement.

"You bet!" Alastair said, casually using some of the American slang he'd learned at boarding school. Eagerly he led the way to where the two big packing crates were tied down to the deck.

It was nightfall by the time the *Luzon Queen* had unloaded its cargo destined for Puerto Princesa, loaded up supplies to deliver to the other towns down the coast, taken on new passengers, and once again headed out of the bay for the open sea. Alastair and Lastani sat on top of the remaining packing crate and watched the lights of the little capital city of Palawan twinkle out, like candles being snuffed, as the steamer headed south.

"What's in that basket Mr. Alvior gave you?" Alastair asked hopefully. He was tired of the sandwiches and raw vegetables the school had packed.

Lastani grinned. "Much good food cooked by Mrs. Alvior." He dug out fresh mangoes, *suman* rice cakes, and even *paella*—rice, shrimp, and chicken wrapped in banana leaves. Alastair dug out his pocketknife and reached for a juicy mango, but Lastani laid a hand on his arm. "We thank Creator God for good food, yes?"

Alastair nodded gratefully. It was good to have a

friend who shared his belief in God. But as Lastani bowed his head and closed his eyes, Alastair was startled to see the piece of carved bone dangling from its leather string beneath the open collar of Lastani's shirt. Doubt pushed its way into his happiness. Why was Lastani still wearing the lambos good-luck charm? Was he just pretending to "go along" with the Christian religion, like Ravi had told him to?

❖ ❖ ❖ ❖

The yard outside the chapel in Brooke's Point was crowded with townspeople—many more than came to worship on Sunday. Word had spread rapidly that the "talking boxes" had arrived, and even those who did not speak Palawano were curious.

Alastair sat on the ground with his mother, sister, and little brothers. "Alastair," whispered Heather, "do you think Papa would let me go with you and Mr. Edwards and Lastani tomorrow when you take the records to his barrio?"

Alastair considered. His sister had been acting very decent lately—none of that boys-are-so-annoying attitude. Why not? She was eleven now. He had been eleven when he first trekked up the mountain. "Just ask," he whispered back.

In the middle of the large circle, Sandy Sutherland and Harry Edwards had set the portable phonograph on a bench from the chapel and placed one of the small records on the turntable.

"I'll turn the crank," Mr. Edwards said to Lastani. "Then you tell the people in English what the record says."

As Sandy Sutherland started to turn the crank, Alastair noticed that some of the Moros tribespeople had joined the crowd at the back of the circle. He recognized Ravi's father from the fish market—and then he saw Ravi, his eyebrows drawn down into a frown.

The record began turning. As Lastani's voice came out of the small megaphone, children giggled and the adults said, "Ahhh." After several sentences, Lastani began translating the Palawano message back into English:

"Men and women needed someone who could take away evil and sin from their hearts and bear their punishment. Finally Chief of Sky came down to this world to do this himself. He became a man. In this form He was called the Son of God. . . ."

Alastair anxiously watched Ravi's face as Lastani "preached" to the crowd about Jesus' death and resurrection. Some of the Muslims were listening intently, but Ravi's frown grew deeper.

Another record was put on, and Lastani translated it also. This one was about the devil, who lied and got men and women to disobey God. "But God loved men and women and wanted them to come back to Him," Lastani translated. Again God's plan of salvation was explained. "The only way to God is by believing in Yesu Krist," Lastani finished. "He is our only Savior."

Lastani's last words were met with a loud, *"No, no, no!"* from the back of the crowd. "This cannot be!" Ravi yelled. "Stop your ears! If we will be continually hearing this, we will come to believe it!"

Alastair saw Lastani look up at the Moros boy whose knife he admired. "It is not so bad to believe, Ravi," the Palawanos boy said with a bold smile, "because it is the truth."

❖ ❖ ❖ ❖

They left before dawn the next day, taking only three of the portable phonographs and three sets of records. The plan was to take the first one to Lastani's barrio—*if* the panglima would give them permission to enter the village. Then Lastani would take the other two to nearby barrios and show the people how to work the simple machine.

The trail was steep, but Alastair noticed that his sister was doing a good job of keeping up. He was glad Papa had let Heather come. After all, she was the one who first said Lastani would make a good translator.

The little party walked single file as they pushed through the thick tangle of vines and ferns that sometimes hid the trail. Alastair looked about uneasily. The last time he had made this trip, someone had tried to kill them with a blowgun. Lastani had said the lambos charm had warned him of danger.

Alastair grabbed a tough bush and pulled himself up a slippery incline. That lambos charm still bothered him. Lastani didn't *act* like he was just pretending about believing in Jesus. He had even told Ravi, right in front of a crowd of people, that it was the truth! But if he really believed in Jesus, why was he still wearing—

"Something bothering you, lad?" said his father's voice. Alastair jumped. He hadn't noticed that his father had dropped back to walk with him.

Alastair hesitated. He had never told anyone about the conversation he'd overheard between Lastani and Ravi. But a quick glance told him the

Palawanos boy was far ahead in the lead, with Heather close behind. Soon he found himself blurting out his doubts to his father.

Sandy Sutherland was thoughtful when Alastair finished. "I don'na think Lastani is pretending," he said. "I think he truly believes. But the lambos charm? God will show him, lad. Be patient. God will show him."

They reached the fork in the trail about noon. Mr. Edwards' carriers put down the boxes that contained the phonographs and records, and they all waited while Lastani went on. Within an hour he was back with Primo. The tribal spokesman seemed excited to see them. "Apo! Hello!" he said. Then he motioned. "Come! Come!"

Now the way got harder. Both Alastair's father and Mr. Edwards helped Heather along. Alastair didn't dare let the person in front of him get out of sight, or the thick forest underbrush would swallow them up.

But finally Primo and Lastani led them into a large barrio hidden away in the lush secrets of Palawan's mountains. Immediately children with long black hair swarmed around them, babbling away in Palawano. Mothers with babies on their hips, wearing nothing but *patadiongs*, skirts of beaten bark, shyly smiled. Soon even the men had gathered, their cheeks full of betel nut.

Alastair noticed Lastani talking to his uncle and the old panglima, pointing to the phonograph that Mr. Edwards was setting up in the middle of the village clearing. A hush fell over the clearing as a record was put on the small phonograph, and Primo turned the hand crank.

Startled cries greeted Lastani's voice as it came out of the small megaphone. "Shh! Shh!" cried Primo. Soon everyone settled down to listen.

This time Lastani did not translate back into English. These people understood Palawano, the language of the record. First one side . . . then the other. Lastani's people listened intently.

Finally they had listened to four records, both sides. Each one a short gospel message. Immediately a clamor went up as the villagers begged to hear them again. But Lastani stood up and walked over to his uncle. With nimble fingers, he untied the leather string around his neck and placed the lambos charm in his uncle's hand, saying something firmly in Palawano.

Sandy Sutherland cocked an eyebrow at Alastair and smiled. As if reading their minds, Lastani turned back to his friends and said, "Lastani does not need good luck anymore. Jesus stronger than evil spirits; Jesus all the protection I need."

Goose bumps crawled along the back of Alastair's neck as Primo put on the first record again and began cranking the handle of the phonograph. Bertie Edwards' dream had come true.

More About Joy Ridderhof

JOY RIDDERHOF HAD BEEN WORKING as a missionary for six years in Central America with the Friends Mission in the 1930s when a severe case of malaria sent her home to Los Angeles. As she lay weakly in bed in her attic room, she fretted about the new converts she had left behind in a remote village in the mountains of Honduras. "If only I could have left my voice behind to encourage them!" she thought.

Memories of the crowded bars in every village, with music blaring from a record player, teased her mind. Everyone in Honduras, it seemed, loved recorded music. What if she made a record with music and the gospel message in Spanish? She was sure the novelty of it would draw a crowd, and the villagers could hear God's Word even when no missionary was present.

Even though weakened by malaria, Joy was nothing if not persistent. What began as a farfetched sickbed idea soon became a reality, and in 1939 Joy had recorded *Buenos Neuvas* ("Good News"), a three-and-a-half minute record. Word spread about Joy's "gospel recording," and missionaries all over Latin America began requesting the records.

But Joy soon realized the importance of using native speakers who were more fluent in the language than she was. Tapping into the various language groups represented in the Los Angeles area, Joy and her former college roommate, Ann Sherwood, made gospel records in Chinese, Spanish, and various Indian dialects. The new ministry soon outgrew Joy's attic bedroom and moved into an old stable that Joy and her friends remodeled. Gospel Recordings was born.

Joy Ridderhof's vision of placing gospel records in remote tribes and villages that did not have the Bible in their own language or where the people could not read would certainly be limited if people who spoke the language had to come to Los Angeles to do the recording. There was only one solution: She had to go to the people.

In 1944, supported by a staff in Los Angeles prepared to produce the recordings and handle mailings, Joy and Ann set out on their first recording trip—a ten-month tour in Mexico and Central America. The travel to remote mountain villages was often difficult for two single women, and the work required endless patience as they searched for a bilingual tribesman who could translate the gospel scripts—oftentimes by simply repeating the words Joy spoke, phrase by phrase. They were hampered by heavy, bulky recording equipment, including a generator to make their own electricity. But they were able to record gospel messages in thirty-five new dialects.

A second trip in 1947 took them to Alaska, visiting remote Indian tribes, where they recorded twenty new languages. In 1949 they sailed for the Philippine Islands—where this story takes place. They relied heavily on missionaries and local pastors to help them locate the necessary tribespeople to make the recordings, sometimes using two or even three different people to translate from English to one language, then from that language into the desired dialect. One recording required 150 splices to get a finished product. But by now their cumbersome recording equipment had given way to the compact, battery-run Minadyk recorder. Even though they spent less than a year in the Philippines, they went home with ninety-two new languages!

On Joy and Ann's fourth recording trip, they were joined by Sanna Barlow and headed for Australia and islands in the Pacific. A fifth recording trip took them to Asia and Africa. It was Sanna Barlow who wrote about many of their adventures in the books listed below.

Meanwhile, other staff members were also being

trained and sent out to do recordings. Back in Los Angeles, the home staff of Gospel Recordings kept busy producing the recordings, stamping records, handling the mailing, and developing new equipment, such as the hand-crank cardboard record player, which had no mechanical parts to break down when left in a remote tribe, and later "The Grip," a simple cassette playback that operated without batteries.

But the traveling teams and the staff back home never got too busy to pray. It was prayer and vision that upheld the ministry no matter what difficulties arose—and Joy Ridderhof's infectious spirit of "Rejoice in all things!" Stories poured in from all over the world of men and women, boys and girls, who heard the message of God's love for the first time and gave their hearts and lives to Jesus because of these gospel recordings.

Even though Joy Ridderhof died in 1984, the work of Gospel Recordings continues. GR offices in over twenty countries continue to produce records in new languages and dialects sent to them by field recordists. To date over 4,900 languages and dialects (out of 8,000 known languages) have been captured on records, taking the Gospel all over the world—all because one woman said "Yes!" to God.

For Further Reading

Thompson, Phyllis. *Count It All Joy!* Wheaton, Ill.: Harold Shaw Publishers, 1978. A biography of Joy Ridderhof and the work of Gospel Recordings around the world.

Barlow, Sanna Morrison. *Mountains Singing.* Chicago: Moody Press, 1960. The Story of Gospel Recordings in the Philippines.

Barlow, Sanna Morrison. *Arrows of His Bow.* Chicago: Moody Press, 1960. The Story of Gospel Recordings in the Solomon Islands.

Barlow, Sanna Morrison. *Light is Sown.* Chicago: Moody Press, 1956. The Story of Gospel Recordings in Africa.

Rossi, Sanna Barlow. *Singing in His Ways: Memoirs of the Joy-Team of Gospel Recordings 1952-1957.* Atlanta: Renewal Enterprises, 1992.

Gospel Recordings' web page at http://user.aol.com/glorenet provides information on the work of Gospel Recordings today, as well as samples of actual recordings that can be played on your computer.

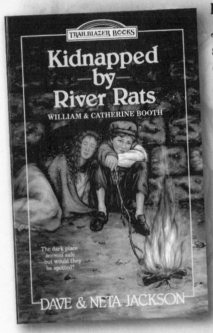